"This must be hard for you," Joshua said.

Mary ducked her head. How could he possibly know how confused and excited she felt when he was near? "Why would seeing you again be hard for me?"

"I meant it must be hard for you to see your community in ruins."

She felt like a fool. "It is sad, but look how everyone is working together. Friends are helping friends. Strangers are helping strangers. It will take a lot of work, but we'll get through this."

"I was wondering if your grandmother's offer of a place to stay was still open? If not, I'm sure I can find another family to put me up."

"Ada and Hannah will be happy to have you stay."

"And you, Mary? Will you be happy if I do?" His voice was low enough that only she could hear him.

She wasn't sure. She was excited at the prospect, and that gave her pause. She already liked him too much. Her track record with liking and trusting the wrong men made her leery of repeating those mistakes.

After thirty-five years as a nurse, **Patricia Davids** hung up her stethoscope to become a full-time writer. She enjoys spending her free time visiting her grandchildren, doing some long-overdue yard work and traveling to research her story locations. She resides in Wichita, Kansas. Pat always enjoys hearing from her readers. You can visit her online at patriciadavids.com.

Books by Patricia Davids

Love Inspired

Brides of Amish Country

Visit the Author Profile page at Harlequin.com for more titles

Amish Redemption

Patricia Davids

HARLEQUIN® LOVE INSPIRED®

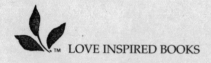

™ LOVE INSPIRED BOOKS

ISBN-13: 978-0-373-81828-0

Amish Redemption

Attend unto my cry; for I am brought very low: deliver me from my persecutors; for they are stronger than I. Bring my soul out of prison, that I may praise thy name: the righteous shall compass me about; for thou shalt deal bountifully with me.

—*Psalms* 142:6–7

The book is lovingly dedicated
to all my readers. Thanks for
making my writing dreams come true.

Chapter One

Joshua Bowman's parole officer turned the squad car off the highway and onto the dirt lane. He stopped and looked over his shoulder. "You want me to drive to the house or do you want to walk from here?"

The immaculate farmstead with the two-story white house, white rail fences and big red barn at the end of the lane had never looked so beautiful. It was like many Amish farms that dotted the countryside around Berlin, Ohio, but this one was special. It was home.

Joshua cleared his throat. "I'd rather walk."

It was kind of Officer Oliver Merlin to allow Joshua's family reunion to take place in private. It was about the only kindness he had received from the *Englisch* justice system. He struggled to put that bitterness behind him. It was time for a new start.

Officer Merlin leveled a hard look at him. "You understand how this works. I'll be back to meet with you in two weeks."

"I'll be here."

"After that, we'll meet once a month until the end of your sentence, but I can drop in anytime. Deliberately miss a meeting with me and you'll find yourself back in prison. I don't take kindly to making long trips for nothing." The man's stern tone left no doubt that he meant what he said.

"I'm never going back there. Never." Joshua voiced the conviction in his heart as he met the officer's gaze without flinching.

"Obey the law and you won't." Getting out of the car, Officer Merlin came around to Joshua's door. There were no handles on the inside. Even though he was on his way home, he was still a prisoner. The moment the door opened, he drew his first free breath in six months.

Freedom beckoned, but he hesitated. What kind of welcome would he find in his father's house?

Officer Merlin's face softened. "I know this is hard, but you can do it, kid."

At twenty-one, Joshua was not a kid, but he appreciated the man's sympathy. He stepped out clutching a brown paper bag that contained his few personal possessions. A soft breeze caressed his cheeks, carrying with it the smells of spring, of the warming earth and fresh green grass. He closed his eyes, raised his face to the morning sun and thanked God for his deliverance.

"See you in two weeks." Officer Merlin closed the door behind Joshua, walked around the vehicle, got in and drove away.

Joshua immediately sat down in the grass at the edge of the road and pulled off his boots and socks. Rising, he wiggled his toes, letting his bare feet relish the cool softness beneath him. Every summer of his life, he had worked and played barefoot along this lane and through these fields. Somehow, it felt right to come home this way. Picking up his bag and carrying his boots in his other hand, he started toward the house.

Set a little way back from the highway stood his father's woodworking shop and the small store where his mother sold homemade candy, jams, jellies, the occasional quilt and the furniture his father and brothers made. The closed sign still hung in the window. His mother would be down to open it as soon as her chores were done.

Joshua had painted the blue-and-white sign on the side of the building when he was fifteen: Bowmans Crossing Amish-Made Gifts and Furniture. At the time, his father thought it was too fancy, but Joshua's mother liked it. The bishop of their congregation hadn't objected, so it stayed. The blue paint was fading. He would find time to touch it up soon. Right now, he had to face his family.

Joshua was a dozen yards from the house when he saw his brothers come out of the barn. Timothy led a pair of draft horses harnessed and ready for working the fields. Noah, the youngest brother, walked beside Timothy. Both big gray horses raised their heads and perked up their ears at the sight of Joshua. One whinnied. His brothers looked to see what had caught their attention.

Joshua stopped. In his heart, he believed he would be welcomed, but his time among the *Englisch* had taught him not to trust in the goodness of others.

Timothy gave a whoop of joy. He looped the reins over the nearby fence and began running toward Joshua with Noah close on his heels. Their shouts brought their oldest brother, Samuel, and their father to the barn door. Samuel broke into a run, too. Before he knew it, Joshua was caught up in bear hugs by first one brother and then the others. Relief made him giddy with happiness, and he laughed out loud.

The commotion brought their mother out of the house to see what was going on. She shrieked with joy and ran down the steps with her white apron clutched in her hands and the ribbons of her Amish prayer *kapp* streaming behind her. She reached her husband's side and grasped his arm. Together they waited.

Joshua fended off his brothers and they fell silent as he walked toward his parents. He stopped a few feet in front of them and braced himself. "I know that I have brought shame and heartache to you both. I humbly ask your forgiveness. May I come home?"

He watched his father's face as he struggled with some great emotion. Tall and sparse with a flowing gray beard, Isaac Bowman was a man of few words. His straw hat, identical to the ones his sons wore, shaded his eyes, but Joshua caught the glint of moisture in them before his father wiped it away. Tears in his father's eyes were something Joshua had never seen before. His mother began weeping openly.

"Willkomme home, *mein sohn."*

Joshua's knees almost buckled, but he managed to stay upright and clasp his father's offered hand. "*Danki*, Father. I will never shame you again."

"There is no shame in what you did. You tried to help your brother. Many of our ancestors suffered unjust imprisonments as you did.

It was God's will." He pulled Joshua forward and kissed him on both cheeks.

When he stepped back, Joshua's mother threw her arms around him. He breathed in the scent of pine cleaner and lemon. Not a day went by that she wasn't scrubbing some surface of her home in an effort to make it clean and welcoming. She had no idea how good she smelled.

Leaning back, she smiled at him. "Come inside. There's cinnamon cake and a fresh pot of *kaffi* on the stove."

"We'll be in in a minute, Mother," Isaac said.

She glanced from her husband to her sons and nodded. "It's so *goot* to have you back."

When she returned to the house, his father began walking toward the barn. Joshua and his three brothers followed him. "Do you bring us news of your brother Luke?"

"He is doing as well as can be expected. I pray that they parole him early, too." It was Luke's second arrest on drug charges, and the judge had given him a longer sentence.

Samuel laid a hand on Joshua's shoulder. "We never believed what they said about you."

"I was in the wrong place at the wrong time. My mistake was thinking that the *Englisch* police would believe me. I thought justice was on the side of the innocent. It's not."

"Do you regret going to Cincinnati to find Luke?" Noah asked.

"*Nee*, I had to try and convince him to come back. I know you said it was his decision, Father, but I thought I could persuade him to give up that wretched life and return with me. We were close once."

In the city, Joshua had discovered his brother had moved from using drugs to making and selling them. Joshua stayed for two days and tried to reason with him, but his pleas had fallen on deaf ears. He'd been ready to accept defeat and return home when the drug raid went down. In a very short time, Joshua found himself in prison alongside his brother. His sentence for a first offense was harsh because his brother had been living near a school.

His father regarded him with sad eyes. "The justice we seek is not of this world, *sohn*. God knows an innocent heart. It is His judgment we must fear."

"Do you think this time in prison will change Luke?" Timothy asked softly.

Prison changed any man who entered those walls, but not always for the better. Joshua shrugged.

His father hooked his thumbs through his suspenders. "You are home now, and for that we must all give thanks. Timothy, Noah, Samuel, the ground will not prepare itself for planting."

Joshua smiled. That was *Daed*—give thanks that his son was home for five minutes and then make everyone get to work.

Joshua's brothers slapped him on the back and started toward the waiting team. Timothy looked over his shoulder. "I want to hear all about the gangsters in the big house tonight."

"I didn't meet any," Joshua called after him, wondering where his brother had picked up such terms.

"Not even one?" Noah's mouth fell open in disbelief.

"Nope." Joshua grinned at his little brother's crestfallen expression. Joshua had no intention of sharing the sights he'd seen in that inhuman world.

"Come. Your mother is anxious to spoil you. She deserves her happiness today."

Joshua followed his father inside. Nothing had changed in the months Joshua had been away. The kitchen was spotless and smelled of cinnamon, fresh-baked bread and stout coffee. Standing with his eyes closed, he let the smells of home wash away the lingering scent of his prison cell. He was truly home at last.

"Sit," his mother insisted.

He opened his eyes and smiled at her. She

wasn't happy unless she was feeding someone. She bustled about the kitchen getting cups and plates and dishing up thick slices of coffee cake. He took a seat at the table, but his father remained by the desk in the corner. He picked up a long white envelope. Turning to Joshua, he said, "Mother's *onkel* Marvin passed away a few months ago."

Joshua frowned. "I don't remember him."

His mother set a plate on the table. "You never met him. He left the Amish as a young man and never spoke to my family again."

"It seems Mother has inherited his property over by Hope Springs." His father tapped the letter against his palm.

"I didn't even know where he lived. His lawyer said he was fond of me because I was such a happy child. Strange, don't you think? Would you like *kaffi* or milk?" she asked with a beaming smile on her face.

"Coffee. What kind of property did he leave you?"

"Forty acres with a house and barn," his father replied. "But the lawyer says the property is in poor repair. I was going to go to Hope Springs the day after tomorrow to look it over, but you know how I hate long buggy trips. Besides, I need to get the ground worked so we can plant. Joshua, why don't you go instead? It would take a load off me, and it would give you a little time to enjoy yourself before getting behind a planter again."

Hope Springs was a day's buggy ride from the farm. The idea of traveling wasn't as appealing as it had once been, but doing something for his father was. "I'd be glad to go for you."

His mother's smile faded. "But Joshua has only just gotten home, Isaac."

Joshua rose to his feet and planted a kiss on her cheek. "You have two whole days to spoil me with your *wunderbar* cooking before then. I'll check out your property, and then I'll be home for good."

"Do you promise?" she asked softly.

He cupped her face in his palms. "I promise."

"Mary, I have just the *mann* for you."

Resisting the urge to bang her head on the cupboard door in front of her, Mary Kaufman continued mixing the lemon cake batter in the bowl she held. "I don't want a man, Ada."

Don't want one. Don't need one. How many ways can I say it before you believe me?

Except for her adopted father, Nick Bradley, most of the men in Mary's life had brought her pain and grief. However, the prospect of finding her a husband was her adopted grandmother's favorite subject. As much as Mary loved Ada, this got old.

"Balderdish! Every Amish woman needs a *goot* Amish husband." Ada opened the oven door.

"The word is *balderdash*."

Ada pulled a cake out using the folded corner of her black apron and dropped it on the stove top with a clatter. "*Mein Englisch* is *goot*. Do not change the subject. You will be nineteen in a few weeks. Do you want people to call you an *alt maedel*?"

"I'll be twenty, and I don't care if people call me an old maid or not."

Ada frowned at her. *"Zvansich?"*

"*Ja*. Hannah just turned four. That means I'll be twenty." Mary smiled at her daughter playing with an empty bowl and wooden spoon on the floor. She was showing her dog, Bella, how to make a cake. The yellow Lab lay watching intently, her big head resting on her paws. Mary could almost believe the dog was memorizing the instructions.

Ada turned to the child. "Hannah, how old are you?"

Grinning at her great-grandmother, Hannah held up four fingers. "This many."

Patting her chest rapidly, Ada faced Mary. "*Ach!* Then there is no time to lose. Delbert

Miller is coming the day after tomorrow to fix the chicken *haus*. You must be nice to him."

Mary slapped one hand to her cheek. "You're right. There's no time to lose. I'll marry him straightaway. If he doesn't fall through that rickety roof and squish all our chickens."

She shook her head and began stirring again. "Go out with Delbert Miller? Not in a hundred years."

"I know he is *en adlichah grohsah mann*, but you should not hold that against him."

Mary rolled her eyes. "A *fairly* big man? *Nee*, he is a *very* big man."

"And are you such a prize that you can judge him harshly?"

Mary stopped stirring and stared at the cuffs of her long sleeves. No matter how hot it got in the summer, she never rolled them up. They covered the scars on her wrists. The jagged white lines in her flesh were indisputable evidence that she had attempted suicide, the ultimate sin. Shame washed over her. "*Nee*, I'm not a prize."

A second later, she was smothered in a hug that threatened to coat her in batter. "Forgive me, child. That is not what I meant. You know that. You are the light in this old woman's heart and your dear *dochder* is the sun and the stars."

Mary closed her eyes and took a deep breath. *God spared my life. He has forgiven my sins.*

I am loved and treasured by the new family He gave me. Bad things happened years ago, but those things gave me my beautiful child. She is happy here, as I dreamed she would be. I will not dwell in that dark place again. We are safe and that evil man is locked away. He can never find us here.

Hannah came to join the group, tugging on Mary's skirt and lifting her arms for a hug, too. Mary set her bowl on the counter and picked up her daughter. "You are the sun and the stars, aren't you?"

"*Ja*, I am." Hannah gave a big nod.

"You are indeed." Ada kissed Hannah's cheek and Mary's cheek in turn. "You had better hurry or you will be late for the quilting bee. I'll finish that batter. Are you taking Hannah?"

"I am. She enjoys playing with Katie Sutter's little ones." Mary glanced at the clock in the corner. It was nearly four. The quilting bee was being held at Katie's home. They were finishing a quilt as a wedding gift for Katie's friend Sally Yoder. Sally planned to wed in the fall.

"Who else is coming?"

"Rebecca Troyer, Faith Lapp, Joann Weaver and Sarah Beachy. Betsy Barkman will be there, of course, and I think all her sisters will be, too."

Betsy Barkman was Mary's dearest friend. They were both still single and neither of them was in a hurry to marry—something few people in their Amish community of Hope Springs understood. Especially Betsy's sisters. Lizzie, Clara and Greta had all found husbands. They were impatiently waiting for their youngest sister to do the same. Betsy had been going out with Alvin Stutzman for over a year, but she wasn't ready to be tied down.

"Sounds like you'll have a wonderful time. Make sure you bring me all the latest gossip."

"We don't gossip." Mary winked at her grandmother.

"*Ja*, and a rooster doesn't crow."

Shifting her daughter to her hip, Mary crossed the room and gathered their traveling bonnets from beside the door. She stood Hannah on a chair to tie the large black hat over her daughter's silky blond crown of braids. As she did, she heard the distant rumble of thunder.

Ada leaned toward the kitchen window to peer out. "There's a storm brewing, from the looks of those clouds. The paper said we should expect strong storms today. You'd better hurry. If it's bad, stay with the Sutters until it passes."

"I will."

"And you will be nice to Delbert when he visits."

"I'll be nice to him. Unless he squashes any of our chickens," Mary said with a cheeky grin.

"Bothersome child. Get before I take a switch to your backside." Ada shook the spoon at Mary. Speckles of batter went everywhere much to Bella's delight. The dog quickly licked the floor clean and sat with her hopeful gaze fixed on Ada.

Laughing, Mary scooped up her daughter and headed out the door. Bella tried to follow, but Mary shook her head. "You stay with *Mammi*. We'll be back soon."

Bella gave her a reproachful look, but turned around and headed to her favorite spot beside the stove.

Mary soon had her good-natured mare harnessed and climbed in the buggy with Hannah. She glanced at the rapidly approaching storm clouds. They did look threatening. The sky held an odd greenish cast that usually meant hail. Should she go, or should she stay home? She hated to miss an afternoon of fun with her friends.

She decided to go. She would be traveling ahead of it on her way to the Sutter farm and Tilly was a fast trotter.

Mary wasted no time getting the mare up to speed once they reached the higaaahway at the end of her grandmother's lane. She glanced back several times in the small rearview mirror on the side of her buggy. The clouds had become an ominous dark shroud, turning the May afternoon sky into twilight. Streaks of lightning were followed by growing rumbles of thunder.

Hannah edged closer to her. "I don't like storms."

She slipped an arm around her daughter. "Don't worry. We'll be at Katie's house before the rain catches us."

It turned out she was wrong. Big raindrops began hitting her windshield a few minutes later. A strong gust of wind shook the buggy and blew dust across the road. The sky grew darker by the minute. Mary urged Tilly to a faster pace. She should have stayed home.

A red car flew past her with the driver laying on the horn. Tilly shied and nearly dragged the buggy into the fence along the side of the road. Mary managed to right her. "Foolish *Englischers*. Have they no sense? We are over as far as we can get."

The rumble of thunder became a steady roar behind them. Tilly broke into a run. Startled, Mary tried to pull her back but the mare struggled against the bit.

"Tilly, what's wrong with you?" She sawed on the reins, trying to slow the animal.

Hannah began screaming. Mary glanced back and her heart stopped. A tornado had dropped from the clouds and was bearing down on them, chewing up everything in its path. Dust and debris flew out from the wide base as the roar grew louder. Mary loosened the reins and gave Tilly her head, but she knew even the former racehorse wouldn't be able to outrun it. They had to find cover.

The lessons she learned at school came tumbling back into her mind: *get underground in a cellar or lie flat in a ditch.*

There weren't any houses nearby. She scanned the fences lining each side of the road. The ditches were shallow to nonexistent. The roar grew louder. Hannah kept screaming.

Dear God, help me save my baby. What do I do?

She saw an intersection up ahead.

Travel away from a tornado at a right angle. Don't try to outrun it.

Bracing her legs against the dash, she pulled back on the lines, trying to slow Tilly enough to make the corner without overturning. The mare seemed to sense the plan. She slowed and made the turn with the buggy tilting on two wheels. Mary grabbed Hannah and held on to her. Swerving wildly behind the horse, the buggy finally came back onto all four wheels. Before the mare could gather speed again, a man jumped into the road, waving his arms.

He grabbed Tilly's bridle as she plunged past and pulled her to a stop.

Shouting, he pointed toward an abandoned farmhouse that Mary hadn't seen back in the trees. "There's a cellar on the south side."

Mary jumped out of the buggy and pulled Hannah into her arms. The man was already unhitching Tilly, so Mary ran toward the ramshackle structure with boarded-over windows and overgrown trees hugging the walls. The wind threatened to pull her off her feet. The trees and even the grass were straining toward the approaching tornado. Dirt and leaves pelted her face, but fear for Hannah pushed her forward. She reached the old cellar door, but couldn't lift it against the force of the wind. She was about to lie on the ground on top of Hannah when the man appeared at her side. Together, they were able to lift the door.

Mary glanced back and saw her buggy flying up into the air in slow motion. The sight was so mesmerizing that she froze.

A second later, she was pushed down the steps into darkness.

Chapter Two

Pummeled by debris in the wind, Joshua hustled the woman and her child down the old stone steps in the hope of finding safety below. He had discovered the cellar that afternoon while investigating the derelict property for his father. He hadn't explored the basement because the crumbling house with its sagging roof and tilted walls didn't look safe. He couldn't believe anyone had lived in it until a few months ago. Now its shelter was their only hope.

The wind tore at his clothes and tried to suck him backward. His hat flew off and out of the steep stairwell to disappear in the roiling darkness overhead. The roar of the funnel was deafening. The cellar door banged shut, narrowly missing his head and then flew open again. A sheet of newspaper settled on the step in front of him and opened gently as if waiting to be read. A second later, the cellar door dropped closed with a heavy thud, plunging him into total darkness.

He stumbled slightly when his feet hit the floor instead of another step. The little girl kept screaming but he barely heard her over the howling storm. It sounded as if he were lying under a train. A loud crash overhead followed by choking dust raining down on them changed the girl's screaming into a coughing fit. Joshua knew the house had taken a direct hit. It could cave in on them and become their tomb instead of their haven.

He pressed the woman and her child against the rough stone wall and forced them to crouch near the floor as he huddled over the pair, offering what protection he could with his body. It wouldn't be much if the floors above them gave way. He heard the woman praying, and he joined in asking for God's protection and mercy. Another crash overhead sent more dust down on them. Choked by the dirt, he couldn't see, but he felt her hand on his face and realized she was offering the edge of her apron for him to cover his nose and mouth. He clutched it gratefully, amazed that she could think of his comfort when they were all in peril. She wasn't screaming or crying as many women would. She was bravely facing the worst and praying.

He kept one arm around her and the child. They both trembled with fear. His actions had helped them escape the funnel itself, but the danger was far from over. She had no idea how perilous their cover was, but he did.

He'd put his horse and buggy in the barn after he arrived late yesterday evening. One look at the ramshackle house made him decide to sleep in the backseat of his buggy while his horse, Oscar, occupied a nearby stall. The barn, although old and dirty, was still sound with a good roof and plenty of hay in the loft. His great-uncle had taken better care of his animals than he had of himself.

Joshua hoped Oscar was okay, but he had no way of knowing if the barn had been spared. Right now, he was more worried that the old house over their heads wouldn't be. Had he brought this woman and her child into a death trap?

Terrified, Mary held Hannah close and prayed. She couldn't get the sight of her buggy being lifted into the sky out of her mind. What if they had still been inside? What if her rescuer hadn't appeared when he did? Was today the day she was to meet God face-to-face? Was she ready?

Please, Father, I beg You to spare us. If this is

*my time to come home to You, I pray You spare
my baby's life. But if You must take Hannah,
take me, too, for I couldn't bear to be parted
from her again.*

The roar was so loud and the pressure so intense that Mary wanted to cover her aching ears, but she couldn't let go of Hannah or the apron she was using to cover their faces. The horrible howling went on and on.

Make it stop, God! Please, make it stop.

In spite of having her face buried in the cloth, thick dust got in her eyes and her nose with every breath. Hannah's small body trembled against her. Her screams had turned to whimpers as her arms tightened around Mary's neck. The roar grew so loud that Mary thought she couldn't take it another moment. Her body shook with the need to run, to escape, to get away.

As soon as the thought formed, the sound lessened and quickly moved on. Was it over? Were they safe?

Thanks be to God.

Mary tried to stand, but the man held her down. "Not yet."

She could hear the wind shrieking and lashing the trees outside, but the horrible pressure in her ears was gone and the roar was fading. In its place, groaning, cracking and thumps reverberated overhead. A thunderous crash shook the ceiling over them and the old timbers moaned. Hannah clutched Mary's neck again. Mary glanced up fearfully. She couldn't see anything for the darkness and the man leaning over her.

He said, "Stay close to the wall. It's the safest place."

She knew what he meant. It was the safest place if the floor above them came down. She huddled against the cold stones, pressing herself and Hannah into as small a space as possible, and waited, praying for herself, her child and the stranger trying to protect them. After several long minutes, she knew God had heard her prayers. The old boards above them stayed intact.

"Is the bad thing gone, *Mamm*?" Hannah loosened her stranglehold on Mary's neck. Her small voice shook with fear.

Mary stroked her hair and kissed her cheek to soothe her. Somewhere in their mad dash, Hannah had lost her bonnet and her braids hung loose. "*Ja*, the bad storm is gone, but keep your face covered. The dust is very thick."

Hannah was only quiet for a moment. "Can we go outside? I don't like it in here."

Mary didn't like it, either. "In a minute, my heart. Now hush."

"We must let the storm pass first," the man said. His voice was deep and soothing. Who was he? In her brief glimpse of him, she had noticed his Amish dress and little else beyond the fact that he was a young man without a beard. That meant he was single, but she didn't recognize him from the area. He was a stranger to her. A Good Samaritan sent by God to aid her in her moment of need. She wished she could see his face.

"Is Tilly okay, *Mamm*?"

"I don't know, dear. I hope so." Mary hadn't spared a thought for her poor horse.

"Who is Tilly?" he asked.

"Our horse," Hannah replied without hesitation, surprising Mary.

Hannah rarely spoke to someone she didn't know. The current situation seemed to have erased her daughter's fear of strange men, or at least this man. It was an anxiety Mary knew she compounded with her own distrust of strangers. She tried to accept people at face value, as good, the way her faith required her to do, but her dealings with men in the past had left scars on her ability to trust as well as on her wrists. Not everyone who gave aid did so without an ulterior motive.

"I think your horse is safe. I saw her running away across the field. Without the buggy to pull, she may have gotten out of the way." There was less tension in his voice. Mary began to relax. The worst was over and they were still alive.

"But Tilly will be lost if she runs off." Hannah's voice quivered.

"*Nee*, a *goot* horse will go home to its own barn," he assured her. "Is she a *goot* horse?"

Mary felt Hannah nod vigorously, although she doubted the stranger could see. "She's a *wunderbar* horse," Hannah declared.

"Then she'll likely be home before you."

Hannah tipped her head to peer at the man. "Did your horse run off, too?"

"Oscar is in the barn. He should be okay in there."

Mary heard the worry underneath his words. In a storm like this, nowhere aboveground was safe.

Hannah rested her head on Mary's shoulder. "Are *Mammi* Ada and Bella okay?"

"They are in God's hands, Hannah. He will protect them." The twister had come up behind them. Mary had no idea if it had touched down before or after it passed over the farm. She prayed for her dear grandmother.

"I want to go home. I want to see *Mammi* Ada and Bella."

"Is Bella your sister?" the man asked.

"She's my *wunderbar* dog."

He chuckled. It was a warm, friendly sound. "Have you a *wunderbar* cat, as well?"

"I don't. Bella doesn't like cats. She's going to be worried about me. We should go home now, *Mamm*." Mary hoped they had a house waiting for them.

"We'll get you home as soon as the storm has moved on," the young man said as he stepped back.

Mary's eyes were adjusting to the gloom. She could see he was of medium height with dark hair, but little else. She knew that without his help things could have been much worse. He could have taken shelter without risking his life to help them. She had his bravery and quick action to thank for getting them out of her buggy before it'd become airborne. Just thinking about what that ride would have been like caused a shiver to rattle her teeth.

He gave her an awkward pat on her shoulder. "I think the worst is over."

She tried not to flinch from his touch. Her common sense said he wasn't a threat, but trusting didn't come easily to her. "We are grateful for your assistance. God was merciful to send you when He did."

He gave a dry bark of laughter. "This time I was in the right place at the right time."

What could he find funny in this horrible situation?

Joshua was amazed at how God had placed him exactly where he needed to be today to save this woman and child, and yet six months ago the Lord had put him in a position that sent him to prison for no good reason. Who could fathom the ways of God? Not he.

"I am Mary Kaufman and this is my daughter, Hannah."

He heard the hesitation in her words and wondered at it. "I'm Joshua Bowman."

"Thank you again, Joshua. Do you think it is safe to venture out?"

A loud clap of thunder rattled the structure over them. "I think we should wait awhile longer."

The thunder was followed by the steady ping of hail against some metal object outside and the drone of hard rain. The tornado had passed but the thunderstorm had plenty of steam left.

"I reckon you're right." Abruptly, she moved away from him.

"I'm sorry. I didn't mean to be overly familiar." Close contact between unmarried members of the opposite sex wasn't permitted in Amish society. Circumstances had forced him to cross that boundary, but it couldn't continue.

"You were protecting us." She moved a few more steps away.

She was uncomfortable being alone with him. He couldn't blame her. She had no idea who he was. How could he put her at ease? Maybe by not hovering over her. He sat down with his back against the old stone wall, refusing to think about the creepy-crawly occupants who were surely in here with them.

She relaxed slightly. "Do you live here?"

"I don't, but my great-uncle did until he died a few months ago."

"I'm sorry for your loss."

"*Danki*, but I never knew him. He was *Englisch*. He left the family years ago and never contacted them again. Everyone was surprised to learn he had willed the property to my mother. She is only one of his many nieces."

"He must have cherished a fondness for her."

"So it would seem. My father sent me to check out the place, as the letter from the attorney said it was in rough shape. *Daed* wants to find out what will be needed to get it ready to farm, rent out or sell. Unfortunately, it's in much worse condition than we expected."

That was an understatement. His father would

have to invest heavily in this farm to get it in working order, and the family didn't have that kind of money. They would need to sell it.

"From the sounds of things, it will need even more repair after the storm passes."

He chuckled at her wry tone. "*Ja.* I think the good Lord may have done us a favor by tearing down the old house. I just wish He had waited until we were out of the way."

His eyes had grown accustomed to the gloom. He could make out Mary's white apron and the pale oval of her face framed by her black traveling bonnet. She sat down, too, pulling her child into her lap. Together, they waited side by side in the darkness. At least she seemed less afraid of him now.

The thunder continued to rumble, punctuating the sound of the wind and the steady rain. They sat in tense silence. Even the child was quiet. After a while, the thunder grew less violent but the rain continued. Was it going to storm all night? If so, he might as well find out what was left of the property and see if he could get this young mother and daughter home.

He rose to his feet. "Stay here until I'm sure it's safe to go out."

She stood, too, holding her little girl in her arms. "Be careful."

He made his way to the cellar door and pushed up on it. It wouldn't budge.

He pushed harder. It still didn't move. Something heavy was blocking it. He worked to control the panic rising in his chest. He couldn't be trapped. Not in such a small place. It was like being in prison all over again. His palms grew damp and his heart began to pound.

"What's wrong?" Mary asked.

The last thing he wanted was to scare her again, but she would soon find out what was going on. He worked to keep his tone calm. There was no point in frightening her more than she already was. "Something is blocking the door. I can't move it. Can you give me a hand?"

He sounded almost normal and was pleased with himself. If she knew differently, she didn't let on. Having someone else to worry about was helping to keep his panic under control.

"Hannah, stay right here," Mary said, then made her way up the steps until she was beside him. She braced her arms against the overhead door. "On three."

She counted off and they both pushed. Nothing. It could have been nailed shut for all their efforts accomplished. He moved a step higher and braced his back against the old boards. He pushed with all his might, straining to move whatever held it. Mary pushed, too, but still the door refused to budge.

This can't be happening.

"Help! Help, we're down here," she yelled, and beat on the door with her fists. He wanted to do the same.

Don't think of yourself. Think of her. Think of her child. They need you to be calm.

He drew a steadying breath. "There isn't anyone around to hear you. This farm has been deserted for months."

"There must be another way out."

He heard the rising panic in her voice. He forced himself to relax and speak casually. "There should be a staircase to the inside of the house. Hopefully, it isn't blocked."

"Of course. Let's find it. I don't want to stay down here any longer than I must. All this dust isn't good for Hannah."

She started to move past him, but he caught her arm. "You could get hurt stumbling around in the dark. Stay here with your daughter. I'll go look. I've got a lighter, but I'm not sure how much fuel is left in it. Shout if you hear anything outside. No one will be looking for me, but your family will be looking for you, right?"

"They will, but not soon."

That wasn't what he wanted to hear. "Maybe

someone will see your buggy out there and come to investigate."

"My buggy isn't out there. Didn't you see it get sucked up and carried away?"

"I didn't. I had my eyes fixed on you."

"No one is going to know where to look for us, are they?" Her voice trembled.

"It won't matter once I find a way out. I'll be back as quick as I can." It was an assurance he didn't really feel.

He tried to remember the layout of the building he had surveyed for his father. Although he had looked in through the windows that hadn't been boarded over, he hadn't ventured inside to explore thoroughly since his father was more interested in the land and its potential. Joshua didn't remember seeing a door that might be an inside entrance to the cellar. Some older houses only had outside entrances. The most logical place for the stairs would be near the kitchen at the other end of the house.

As it continued to rain, water began pouring through cracks in the floorboards overhead. That wasn't good. It meant a part of the house had been torn open, allowing the rain to come in. How sound was what remained? The steady rumble of thunder promised more rain. Would the saturated wood give way and finish what the tornado had started? He looked over his shoulder. "Mary, stay near the wall or in the stairwell, okay?"

"I will."

Joshua surveyed what he could in the darkness. The cellar itself wasn't empty. The only clear place seemed to be where they were standing. The cavernous space was piled high with odds and ends of lumber, boxes, old tires and discarded household items. His great-uncle, it seemed, had been a hoarder as well as a recluse.

Joshua had put a lighter in his pocket before leaving the farm in case he ended up camping out. It had come in handy last night and now he pulled it out, clicked it on and held it over his head. Gray cobwebs waved from every surface in the flickering light that did little to pierce the gloom. He couldn't keep the lighter on for long before he burned his fingers, so he quickly identified a path and let the light go out.

Stepping around a pair of broken chairs, he pushed aside wooden boxes of unknown items. When his shin hit something, he flicked on the lighter again. A set of box springs blocked his way. Most of the cloth covering had rotted away. Mice had made off with more. Skirting it as best he could without stepping on the springs, he continued along the cellar wall. A set of shelves on the far side was lined with dust-covered cans, jars and crocks, but he saw no stairs. He finished the circuit and moved back toward where Mary was standing. He flicked on his light.

"Have you discovered a way out?" Her voice shook only slightly, but he saw the worry in her eyes.

They weren't going anywhere until someone found them. He had no idea how long that might take. They could be down here for hours, days even. The thought was chilling. He stopped a few feet away from her and let the light go out. How did he tell a frightened woman she was trapped in a cellar with a man who'd spent the past six months in prison?

When Joshua didn't answer her question, Mary's heart sank. She knew he hadn't found an exit. She bit her thumbnail as she considered their predicament. Her friends would be concerned when she didn't arrive at the quilting bee, but they might assume she had stayed home to wait out the storm. When she didn't return home this evening, Ada would become concerned, but she might think Mary had decided to spend the night at the Sutter farm. Ada might not even know about the tornado if it had formed this side of the farm.

Mary hoped that was the case. Ada had a bad heart and didn't need such worry. It could be morning before she became concerned about them and perhaps as late as noon before she realized they were missing.

Mary's adoptive parents, Nick and Miriam Bradley would begin looking for them as soon as their absence was noted. Miriam stopped at the farm every morning and Nick dropped by every evening on his way home from work without fail. He would know about the tornado. He would stop by the farm this evening to make sure she and Hannah were safe. Would he go to the Sutter farm to check on them when he found they weren't home? She had no way of knowing, but she prayed that he would.

It might take a while, but Nick would find them. Mary had no doubt of that. But would he find them before dark? Or was she going to have to spend the night with this stranger?

Chapter Three

Mary shivered as she looked around the old cellar. If she had to spend the night in here, she wouldn't like it, but she could do it. She would depend on God for His protection and comfort. In the meantime, she had to be brave for her child and make the best of a bad situation for Joshua's sake, too. He was trying to hide his fear, but she saw it in his eyes.

"I noticed an old lantern hanging from a nail by the cellar steps. We should check and see if it has any kerosene in it." She spoke calmly, surprised to find her voice sounded matter of fact.

"Good idea. I'll see if I can find an ax or something useful to chop open or pry up the door." Joshua flicked his lighter on. He located the lantern, took it down from the nail and shook it. A faint sloshing sound gave Mary hope.

Hannah tugged on her skirt. "I'm hungry. Can we go home now?"

Joshua leaned toward her. "You mean you want to go home before our adventure has ended?"

Hannah gave him a perplexed look. "What adventure?"

"Why, our treasure hunt." He raised the glass chimney of the lantern and held his lighter to the wick. It flickered feebly for a second and then caught. He lowered the glass, wiped it free of dust with his sleeve and turned up the wick. The lamp cast a golden glow over their surroundings. It was amazing how much better Mary felt now that she could see.

"What kind of treasure hunt?" Hannah sounded intrigued by the idea.

"We're all going to hunt for some useful things," Mary said.

Joshua nodded. "That's right. Let's pretend that we are going to make this cellar into a home. What do we need first?"

"Chairs and a table," Hannah said.

"Then help me look for some on our pretend shopping trip." He glanced at Mary. She nodded and he held out his hand to Hannah. "I think I saw some chairs over this way. Don't you like to go shopping? I do. This storekeeper needs to sweep out his store, though. This place is as dirty as a rainbow."

Hannah scowled at him. "Rainbows aren't dirty. They're pretty and clean."

He held his lantern higher. "Are they? Well, this place isn't. It's as dirty as a star."

"Stars aren't dirty, Joshua. They twinkle."

"Then you tell me what is dirty."

"A pigpen."

"Yup, that is dirty, all right, but this place is worse than a pigpen. What else is dirty?"

"Your face."

Mary choked on her laugh. Hannah was right. His face was covered in dirt. There were cobwebs on his clothes and bits of leaves and grass in his dark brown hair. It was then she realized how short his hair was. It wasn't the style worn by Amish men. Joshua must still be in his *rumspringa*.

Mary had left her running-around years behind a few short weeks after Hannah was born. She had been baptized into the Amish faith at the age of sixteen, the time when most Amish teens were just beginning to test the waters of the English world.

Joshua seemed to notice she was staring at him. He rubbed a hand over his head in a self-conscious gesture and shook free some of the clinging grime.

Mary looked away. She wiped down her sleeves and brushed off her bonnet, knowing she couldn't look much better. Oddly, she wished she had a mirror to make sure her face was clean. It wasn't like her to be concerned with her looks, but she did wonder what Joshua thought of her.

That was silly. He would think she was a married woman with a child, and that was a good thing. She glanced at him again.

He wiped his face with both hands but it didn't do much good. He spoke to Hannah. "This isn't dirt. It's flour. I was going to bake a cake."

Hannah giggled at his silliness. "It is not flour."

"Okay, but this is a table and we need one." He held his find aloft. The ancient rocker was missing a few spindles in the back, but the seat was intact.

Hannah planted her hands on her hips. "That's a chair."

"It's a good thing I have you to help me shop. I'd never find the right stuff on my own. Let's go look for a donkey."

Hannah giggled again. "Joshua, we don't need a donkey in our house."

"We don't? I'm so glad. I don't know where it would sleep tonight."

His foolishness made Mary smile. He was

distracting and entertaining Hannah. For that, she was grateful. Mary turned her attention to finding something to collect the rainwater. She had no idea how long they might be down here, but Hannah was sure to be thirsty soon.

She found a metal tub hanging from a post near the center of the room. It had probably been a washtub at one time. Using her apron, she wiped it out and positioned it under the worst of the dripping. Next, she found an empty glass canning jar and rinsed it out the same way. She put it in the center of the tub. Once the jar was full, the overflow would accumulate in the tub and leave her something to wash with later.

The plink, plink, plink of the water hitting the bottom of the jar was annoying, but they would be grateful for the bounty before morning. She refused to think they might be down here more than one night.

Taking off her bonnet, she laid it aside. Then she held the cleanest corner of her apron under a neighboring drip until it was wet and unobtrusively used it to scrub her face.

At the end of their shopping trip, Joshua and Hannah came back with two barely usable chairs, a small wooden crate for a third seat and another washtub with a hole in the side for a table, but no ax or tools. Joshua set the furniture up in their corner, allowing Hannah to arrange and rearrange them to her satisfaction in her imaginary house.

While her daughter was busy, Mary spoke quietly to Joshua. "I will be fine until we are rescued, but Hannah will be hungry soon. Do you have anything to eat?"

"Nothing. I'm sorry. Everything I have is out in my buggy in the barn. There are some cans and jars on the shelf back there. Want me to take a look?"

"*Nee*, you're doing a wonderful job keeping Hannah occupied. I'll go look." Normally leery of strangers, Mary didn't feel her usual disquiet with Joshua. She assumed their current circumstances made him seem like less of a stranger and more like a friend in need.

He pulled a candle stub from his pocket. "I found this along with a couple of others in a pan. It was the best one." He lit it, dripped a small amount of wax on the overturned washtub and stuck the butt in it to hold the candle upright. Then he handed Mary the lantern.

"Someone was probably saving them to melt down to reuse." She didn't have a mold to form a new candle, but she could make one by dipping a wick in the melted wax. A strip of cotton cloth from her apron or from her *kapp* ribbon would make an adequate wick. She would work on that before the lantern ran out of fuel. Sitting in the dark was the last thing she wanted to do.

Hannah began jumping up and down. "I hear a siren. Do you hear it? It's Papa Nick!"

Mary's spirits rose until the welcome sound faded away. Nick wasn't coming for them. He had no idea where she was. It might not even have been him. How much damage had been done by the tornado? Were others in need of rescue?

A few moments later, she heard the sound of another siren on the highway. Were they ambulances rushing to help people injured by the twister? She had been praying so hard for herself and for Hannah that she had forgotten about others in the area. This part of the county was dotted with English and Amish farms and businesses. How many had been destroyed? How many people had lost their lives? She prayed now for all the people she knew beyond the stone walls keeping her prisoner. It was the only thing she could do to help.

Lifting the lantern, she moved across the crowded room to the shelves Joshua had indicated and searched through the contents. She glanced back to see him placing the tub as Hannah instructed in her imaginary house. The lantern flickered and Mary turned up the wick. She hated being trapped, but at least she didn't have to face the situation alone.

A dozen times in the next half hour the eerie wailing of sirens rose and fell as they passed by on the highway a quarter of a mile away from the house. Each time, Mary's hopes sprang to life and then ebbed away with the sound. She met Joshua's eyes. They both knew it was a bad sign.

Joshua noticed the growing look of concern on Mary's face. It didn't surprise him. He was concerned, too. He had no idea when rescue would come. Would anyone think to search an old house that had been abandoned for months? Why would they? He racked his brain for a way to signal that they were here, but came up empty. Someone would have to come close enough to hear them shouting.

Hannah came to stand in front of him with her hands on her hips. "Joshua, we need a stove and a bed now. Take me shopping again."

She looked and sounded like a miniature version of her mother. He had to smile. "You are a bossy woman. Does your mother boss your *daed* that way?"

Hannah shook her head. "He died a long time ago. I don't remember him. But I have Papa Nick."

At first, Joshua had assumed Papa Nick was *Englisch* because Hannah connected him to the siren she heard. However, the siren could have belonged to one of the many Amish volunteer fire department crews that dotted the area. Was Papa Nick her new father, perhaps? He glanced to where Mary was searching the shelves and asked quietly, "Who is Nick?"

"He's my papa Nick," the child said, as if that explained everything.

"Is he your mother's husband?"

"Nee." She laughed at the idea.

He glanced at Mary with a new spark of interest. She wasn't married, as he had assumed. It was surprising. Why would the men in this community overlook such a prize? Perhaps she was still mourning her husband. Joshua rubbed his chin. He noticed a bit of cobweb dangling from his fingers and shook it off. He needed to concentrate on getting out of this cellar, not on his interest in Hannah's mother.

He patted Hannah's head. "We will go shopping as soon as your *mamm* returns. Let's wait and see if she brings us any treasures."

"Okay." Hannah sat on her makeshift chair, put her elbows on her knees and propped her chin in her hands. "I wish Bella was here."

Joshua sat gingerly in the chair with a broken arm. He sighed with relief when it held his weight. Remembering the black-and-white mutt that had been his inseparable companion when he was only a little bit older than Hannah, he asked, "What kind of dog is she?"

"She's a yellow dog."

Joshua smothered a grin and managed to say, "They're the best kind."

"Yup. She was *Mammi* Miriam's dog, but when I was born, Bella wanted to belong to me."

Mary returned with several jars in her hand. "These pears are still sealed and the rings were taken off so they aren't rusty. If worst comes to worst, we can try them, but they are nearly three years old from what I can read of the labels."

He grimaced. "Three-year-old pears don't sound appetizing."

"I wasn't suggesting they were, but I've known people to eat home-canned food that was older than this."

"Really? How can you tell if it's bad?"

"If the seal is intact, if the food looks good and smells okay, it should be okay…" Her voice trailed off.

He folded his arms over his chest. "You go first."

She rolled her eyes and he smiled. He could have been trapped with a much less enjoyable companion. "Come on, Hannah. We're going shopping for a bed. I think I saw one earlier that might go with our decor."

"What's decor?" Hannah asked, jumping off her chair.

He gestured toward his clothing. "It means style."

"What is your style?" Mary asked with a gleam of amusement in her eyes.

"Cobwebs and dust. What's yours?" He leaned toward her. "How did you get your face clean?"

She blushed and looked down. "There is plenty of water dripping in on the other side. You could wash up if you'd like."

"Good idea. Come on, Hannah. Let's get some of this decor off of us."

"*Ja*, it's yucky."

Mary stopped Hannah. She lifted the girl's apron off over her head, tore it in two and handed him the pieces. "Use this to wash and dry with. It's the cleanest thing you'll find down here."

"*Danki.*" As he took it from her, his fingers brushed against hers, sending a tiny thrill across his skin. She immediately thrust her hands in the pockets of her dress and her blush deepened.

She was a pretty woman. He liked the way wisps of her blond hair had come loose from beneath her *kapp* and curled around her face. He liked her smile, too. Would he have noticed her if they hadn't been forced together? In truth, he wouldn't have looked twice if he saw her with a child. He realized he was staring and turned away. The last thing he wanted was for her to feel uncomfortable.

After washing Hannah's face and his own, Joshua returned to find Mary had put the candle stubs he'd seen in a small jar. She was melting them over the flame of the candle on the tub. Hannah had found a worn-out broom with a broken handle. She began using it to sweep the floor of her house. "We didn't find a stove, *Mamm*."

Joshua gestured toward Mary's jar. "Are you going to make me eat wax for supper because I don't want your ancient pears?"

Using a piece of broken glass, she cut the ribbons off her *kapp*. "*Nee*, I'm making more candles."

"Smart thinking." The lantern had been flickering. It would go out soon and he hadn't found more kerosene.

She flashed him a shy smile before looking down. "I have my moments."

He noticed she had opened one of the jars of fruit. "Did you eat some of that?"

She nodded. "If I don't get sick, it should be fine for the two of you."

"I'm not sure that was smart thinking. Were they good?"

"As sweet as the day they were canned, but kind of mushy. Would you like some?"

"I'll pass. I might have to take care of you if you get sick. Besides, I'm not hungry."

She glanced up. "I feel fine. Did you find a bed for Hannah?"

He sat down in the chair. "Just some rusty box springs and a pile of burlap sacks. I'll bring them over later. It's not much, but it will have to do. I'm sorry I couldn't find anything for you."

"The rocker will suit me fine." She dipped her ribbon in the melted wax and pulled it out. Letting it harden, she waited a little while and then dipped it again. Each time she pulled it out, the candle grew fatter. Hannah came over and Mary allowed her to start her own candle.

It was pleasant watching them work by lantern light. Mary was patient with her daughter, teaching her by showing her what to do and praising her when she did well. Outside, the sound of rain faded away. The storm was over. Would someone find them soon?

"You mentioned you were here inspecting the property. Where is home?"

He gingerly settled back in his chair. "My family has a farm and a small business near a place called Bowmans Crossing. It's north and west of Berlin."

"Do you have a big family?" Hannah asked.

"Four brothers, so not very big."

Hannah gave a weary sigh. "I want a brother *and* a sister, but *Mamm* says no."

Joshua chuckled.

Mary refused to look at him. "You have Bella. That's enough."

He couldn't resist teasing her. "Your *mamm* needs a husband first, Hannah."

Hannah's eyes widened and she held up a hand. "That's what *Mammi* Ada says. She says *Mamm* will turn into an old *maedel* if we don't find her a husband soon."

Joshua tipped his head to the side as he regarded Mary's crimson cheeks. "I think she has a few years yet. Tell your grandmother not to worry."

"I wish you two would stop talking about me as if I weren't here. Your candle is thick enough, Hannah. I think Joshua should make up a bed for you."

Hannah looked at her in shock. "You mean we have to sleep here?"

Mary cupped her daughter's cheek. "I'm afraid so."

"I sure wish this adventure was over. Can I have supper now?"

Mary glanced at Joshua. He shrugged. "If you feel okay, I don't see why not."

Hannah enjoyed eating sticky pear halves

with her fingers while Joshua fixed a makeshift bed for her. It wasn't much, but it would keep her off the cold damp floor. She made a face as she crawled onto the burlap bags. Mary checked the edge of her apron and found it was dry now. She pulled it off and used it to cover Hannah. It wasn't long before the child was asleep. The lamp died a few minutes later.

Joshua lit the candle that Mary had made and stuck it to the middle of the tub. It would burn out long before the night was over. Mary settled in the rocker, but he knew she didn't sleep any better than he did. The long night crawled past. He had no way to tell time. He simply had to endure the darkness, as he had done in prison.

The distant rumble of thunder woke him some time later. He lifted his head and winced at the pain in his neck. Opening his eyes, he realized he was still in the cellar. It was dark, but he could make out Mary's form in the other chair.

She sat forward and bent her neck slowly from side to side. "Is it morning?"

"I think so."

"It's raining again."

"Ja."

"I was dreaming about bacon and eggs."

His stomach rumbled. "I was dreaming about three-year-old pears."

"Really?"

"*Nee*, I wasn't dreaming at all. If I was, I'd wake up and find I was at home in my own bed."

"Wouldn't that be nice?"

They both stood and stretched. She looked at him. "What's the plan for today?"

He rubbed his bristly cheeks with both hands. "I thought you had a plan."

"I'm sure it's your turn to come up with something. I thought of making the candles."

He nudged the broken rocker with his boot. "Which was good, but I thought of finding furniture for our snug little home. It's your turn to be brilliant."

"I've never felt less brilliant in my life. What would you like for breakfast? I believe we have more three-year-old pears or some four-year-old peaches."

"Peaches," Hannah said, sitting up on her makeshift mattress.

"Peaches," he agreed. "Provided they look safe."

After their meal, they spent more time exploring for a way out without success. By noon, the rain had moved on and a few narrow beams of sunlight streamed through cracks in the floorboards overhead, allowing them to see their dismal surroundings a little better.

Joshua studied the cracks for a while. "I think I might be able to knock some of the floor planks loose if I can find something sturdy to reach them."

"I knew you would have a plan." Mary began to search through the piles of junk and he joined her.

The best thing he could come up with was a post about five feet long and two inches thick. He chose a spot overhead, wrapped some cloth around one end of the wood to prevent slivers and began thrusting it upward. Mary and Hannah stood nearby watching him. After half an hour, his arms were aching, the end of the post was beginning to splinter and the floorboard above him had only been displaced by an inch. It was something, but it wasn't enough.

Mary reached for his battering ram. "Let me work on it for a while. Do you think we'd do better to try and knock a hole in the cellar door?"

He handed her the wooden post. "It's reinforced with metal straps and I didn't see any light shining in through it. There's no telling what's on top of it. I know it's open above me here."

They took turns working for several hours and had the ends of two planks above them loose when Mary suddenly grabbed his arm. "Wait. Stop. I hear a dog."

The barking grew louder.

Hannah got up off the floor and began jumping. "I hear Bella."

Joshua gave a mighty heave and the floorboard broke, leaving a narrow space open. They looked at each other. "Neither of us can fit through that," he said, his excitement ebbing away.

"Hannah might be able to."

The sunlight dimmed and Joshua looked up. The head of a large yellow dog was visible above him. The dog barked excitedly. Hannah rushed to Joshua's side. "I knew I heard Bella."

"I hear voices, too." Mary began shouting. A few moments later, the dog was pushed aside.

An English woman with brown hair knelt down to look in. "Mary, is that you? Is Hannah with you?"

Tears of joy streamed down Mary's face. "We're okay, Miriam, but we can't get the cellar door open."

"Thank God you are safe. We'll get you out. Don't worry. Nick, I found them!" She disappeared from view. The dog came back to the opening. She lay down and woofed softly.

Mary threw her arms around Joshua in an impulsive hug. "I knew they would find us. I just knew it."

Bella barked again. As if Mary realized what she was doing, she suddenly stepped away from

Joshua and crossed her arms. "It's Miriam and Nick, my adoptive parents. Nick will get us out of here."

Joshua heard activity at the door and the sounds of something heavy being dragged aside. "Looks like our prayers have been answered."

Mary picked up Hannah. Joshua followed them as they hurried to the stairwell.

From the other side, a man said, "Everyone stand clear."

"We are, Nick." Mary replied. The sound of an ax striking the portal was followed by splintering wood. A hole appeared in the top of the door and grew rapidly. Through it, Joshua could see the leaves and limbs of a large tree that must have been holding the door shut. Mary's father was swinging the ax like a madman. Joshua ached to help, but he could only stand by and wait.

Finally, the top section of the door broke free and a man's hands reached in. "Give me Hannah."

Mary handed the child over and then waited until the opening was enlarged. Joshua boosted her up and then climbed out on his own. The sunshine and the fresh air was a blessed relief from their dark, dank room. He blinked in the brightness and focused on Hannah in the arms of a woman in her early thirties. Mary was in the embrace of a man in a brown uniform. It wasn't until he released her that Joshua realized he was an *Englisch* lawman.

Mary turned to him with a bright smile, but he couldn't smile back. "Joshua, this is my adopted father, Sheriff Nick Bradley."

A knot formed in the pit of Joshua's stomach as dread crawled up his spine.

Chapter Four

Mary's father was the *Englisch* sheriff!

It was all Joshua could do to stand still. He hadn't done anything wrong, but that hadn't made any difference the last time he'd had a run-in with the law. Cold sweat began trickling down his back.

"The storm came up so suddenly. I didn't know what to do when I saw the funnel cloud. Then Joshua stopped Tilly and pulled us into the cellar. God put him there to rescue us." Mary was talking a mile a minute until she turned to look at the house. Her eyes widened.

Joshua turned, too. Only part of one wall had been left standing. The rest was a pile of jagged, splinted wood, broken tree limbs, scattered clothing and old appliances. A small round table sat in one corner of what must have been a bedroom. There was a book and a kerosene lamp still sitting on it. The remainder of the room had been obliterated.

Hannah reached for Nick. He took the child from Miriam, who promptly drew Mary into her embrace.

"We're so thankful you're safe. God bless you, Joshua." Miriam smiled her thanks at him.

Hannah threw her arms around Nick's neck. "I'm so happy to see you, Papa Nick."

"I'm happy to see you, too, Hannah Banana," he said, patting her back, his voice thick with emotion.

She drew back to frown at him. "I'm not a banana."

He smiled and tweaked her nose. "You're not? Are you sure?"

She giggled. "I'm a girl."

"Oh, that's right."

It was apparently a running gag between the two, because they were both grinning. The sheriff put Hannah down and held out his hand to Joshua. "Pleased to meet you. My heartfelt thanks for keeping my girls safe."

Joshua reluctantly shook the man's hand and hoped the sheriff didn't notice how sweaty his palms were. "No thanks are necessary."

Nick's eyes narrowed slightly. "You aren't from around here, are you? I didn't catch your last name."

Here it comes. Joshua braced himself. "Bowman. My family is from over by Berlin."

"The name rings a bell. Who is your father?" Nick tilted his head slightly as he stared at Joshua intently.

"Isaac Bowman." Joshua held his breath as he waited to be denounced as a criminal. What would Mary think of her rescuer then? He wasn't sure why it mattered, but it did.

Miriam lifted Hannah into her arms. "Stop with the interrogation, Nicolas. Let's get these children someplace safe. We still have a lot of work to do."

"Is Ada okay?" Mary asked, looking to Miriam.

Nodding, Miriam said, "She's fine except for being worried about you and Hannah. The house was only slightly damaged, but her corncribs were destroyed."

"Oh, no. Who else was affected? We heard the sirens last evening."

Miriam and Nick exchanged speaking glances. Nick said, "A lot of people. The Sutters' house was damaged. Elam has minor injuries. Katie, the kids and the women who were gathered for the quilting bee are all okay. I'm sorry to tell you that Bishop Zook was seriously injured. They took him to the hospital last night and into surgery this morning. We're still waiting for word about him. He lost his barn and his house was heavily damaged, but his wife is okay."

"Oh, dear." Mary's eyes filled with tears. Miriam hugged her.

Nick cleared his throat. "The tornado went straight through the south end of Hope Springs. Ten blocks of the town were leveled. We're only beginning to assess the full extent of the damage in the daylight. I need to get back there. We've still got a search-and-rescue effort underway. As of noon, we had seven people unaccounted for, but that goes down to five now that we've found you and Hannah."

Mary took Hannah from Miriam. "How did you find us? We were supposed to be at the Sutter place."

Nick said, "When Ada saw your mare come home without you, she got really worried. She walked to a neighbor's house to use their phone to call me last night. We checked with Katie and learned you never arrived. Your buggy was found in Elam Sutter's field at first light this morning. When we saw you weren't in it, we picked up Bella in the hopes that she could locate you and tried to retrace your path. She led us here."

"She must have heard us pounding. She

couldn't have followed our scent after all that rain," Mary said.

"I don't know how she knew, but she did." Miriam patted the dog and then began walking toward the road, where a white SUV sat parked at the intersection with its red lights flashing. The sheriff followed her.

Grateful that he hadn't been outed, Joshua caught Mary's arm, silently asking her to remain a moment. She did. Their brief time together was over and he needed to get going. "I'm glad things turned out okay for you and Hannah."

"Only by God's grace and because you were here."

"You were very brave, Mary. I want you to know how much I admire that. You're a fine mother and a good example for your daughter. I'm pleased to have met you, even under these circumstances."

She blushed and looked down. "I have been blessed to meet you, too, and I shall always count you among my friends."

"I need to get going. My folks are expecting me home in a day or two. When they hear about this storm they'll worry." He took a step back.

Mary's eyes grew round as she looked past him. "Oh, no."

"What?" He turned and saw the barn hadn't been spared. Half of it was missing and the rest was leaning precariously in hay-covered tatters. He'd been so shaken to see the sheriff that he had forgotten about his horse. He started toward what was left of the building at a run.

Mary was tempted to follow Joshua, but she knew he might need more help than she could provide. Instead, she ran after Nick. She caught up with him and quickly explained the situation.

Nick said, "I'll help him. Let Miriam drive you and Hannah home and then she can come back for me."

"Absolutely not," Miriam said before Mary could answer. "I'm not leaving until you and that young man are both safe."

He kissed her cheek. "That's why I love you. You never do what I tell you. Call headquarters and let them know what's going on. I don't want them to think I've gone on vacation."

"I will. Be careful."

As Nick jogged toward the barn, Mary said, "I'm going to see what I can do."

"No, the men can manage."

"More hands will lighten the load." Mary raced after Nick. When she reached the teetering edge of the barn, she hesitated. She couldn't see what was holding it up as she slowly made her way inside the tangled beams and splintered wood. Everything was covered with hay that had spilled down from the loft. It could be hiding any number of hazards.

Once she reached the interior, she no longer had to scramble over broken wood, so the going was easier. She saw the flattened remains of Joshua's buggy beneath a large beam. Ominous creaking came from overhead. Joshua and Nick were pulling debris away from one of the nearby stalls. A section of the hayloft had collapsed like a trapdoor, blocking their way. She reached Joshua's side and joined him as he pulled at a stubbornly lodged board.

He stopped what he was doing and scowled at her. "Get out of here right now."

"You don't get to tell me what to do." She yanked on the board and it came free. She tossed it behind her.

Joshua turned to Nick. "Tell her it isn't safe."

"It isn't safe, Mary," Nick said.

"It is safe enough for you two to be in here." She lifted another piece of wood and threw it aside.

"See what I have to put up with, Joshua? None of the women in my family listen to me."

Mary heard a soft whinny from inside the stall. "Your horse is still alive, Joshua."

He said, "We're coming, Oscar. Be calm, big fella."

They all renewed their efforts and soon had a

small opening cleared. The gap was only wide enough for Mary to slip through. Joshua's horse limped toward her. He had a large cut across his rump and down his hip.

"Oh, you poor thing." Mary stroked his face. He nuzzled her gently.

"How is he?" Joshua asked.

"He has a bad gash on his left hip, but the bleeding has stopped. How are we going to get him out of here?"

Nick said, "Even if we free him from the stall, he can't climb over the debris to get out the way we came in."

"Can you cut through the outside wall?" To her, it looked like the fastest way out.

"The silo came down on that side and left a few tons of bricks in the way."

Looking around from inside the stall, Mary saw only one other likely path. "If you can get into the next stalls and pull down the walls between them and this one, we could lead him through to the outside door at the far end of the building."

"It's worth a look," Nick said.

He and Joshua headed in that direction. She heard Joshua call to her. "Mary, if the upper level starts shifting, I want you to leave the horse and get out as fast as you can."

"I will," she called back. She patted Oscar's

dusty brown neck and said softly, "Don't worry. We'll get out of this together."

The sound of her father's ax smashing into wood told her they were starting. She looked up, ready to scurry through the gap if she had to.

She hadn't been waiting long when the chopping stopped. She heard voices but couldn't make out what they were saying. Oscar whinnied. From outside, more horses answered. The sound of a chain saw sent her spirits soaring. Someone had joined Nick and Joshua.

It took less than five minutes before she saw her new rescuer cutting through the adjoining stall. It was Ethan Gingerich, a local Amish logger. Oscar began shifting uneasily. She realized he was frightened by the sound and smell of the chain saw. He tried to rear in the small space with her. She barely had room to avoid his hooves.

"Ethan, wait! He's too fearful."

Ethan killed the saw's engine. Oscar quieted, but he was still trembling. Mary patted his neck to reassure him and spoke soothingly.

"Use this to cover his eyes." Ethan, a bear of a man, unbuttoned the dark vest he wore over his blue shirt, slipped it off and handed it to Joshua. Joshua climbed over the half wall with ease and quickly tucked the vest into Oscar's halter, making sure the horse couldn't see any light. Although the horse continued to tremble, he didn't move. Without the roar of the saw, Mary could hear creaking and groaning from the remains of the hayloft.

Joshua kept his hold on Oscar and gave Mary a tired smile. "I've got him now. Thanks for your help. You would be doing me a great favor if you went outside."

His shirt was soaked with sweat and covered with sawdust and bits of straw. He'd been working to the point of exhaustion to get to her, not just to his horse. She nodded and watched relief fill his eyes. "I reckon I can do that."

He moved closer to the half wall and bent his knee. She stepped up and swung her leg over the wide boards. Nick caught her around the waist and lifted her down. She brushed off her skirt, straightened her *kapp* and went down the length of the barn through the openings they had cut. Behind her, she heard the chain saw roar to life again. She was tempted to stop and make sure all the men got out safely, but she knew they didn't need her.

Outside, she saw Miriam standing a few yards away beside the team of huge draft horses that belonged to Ethan. She had Hannah by the hand. When Hannah saw her, she dropped Miriam's hand and raced forward. "*Mamm*, Bella chased a rabbit into the field and she won't come back. I called her and called her."

"That naughty dog." She swung Hannah up into her arms.

Miriam crossed her arms and glared at Mary. "Bella is not the only naughty member of this family. Go wait for us in the car, Hannah."

Mary put her daughter down and watched her run to the vehicle. Hannah loved to ride in Papa Nick's SUV. He often let her play with the siren. Smiling, Mary turned back to Miriam, but her adoptive mother's face was set in stern lines. Mary sought to defend herself. "I had to help. You would have done the same."

"No, I wouldn't have. They could have managed without you. You have a kind but impulsive nature, Mary. It's better to think things through than to rush into something only to find bigger trouble. You should know that better than anyone. Nick wouldn't have come out of there without you no matter how dangerous it became. He would have left the horse if he had to."

Miriam almost never scolded her, and she never brought up Mary's past. Chastised, Mary stared at the ground and whispered, "I'm sorry."

She felt Miriam's hand on her shoulder. "I know you are. I just want you to think with your head and not let your emotions rule you. Just be more cautious."

Mary heard trepidation in Miriam's voice. She was more upset than Mary's action warranted. "I'm sorry I frightened you. You must have been worried sick all night long."

Miriam pulled her close. "I was. Promise me you'll be more careful."

"I promise."

When Miriam held her tighter and didn't release her, Mary knew something else was troubling her mother. "What's wrong?"

Miriam sighed. "I didn't want to tell you this now after all you've been through, but there is something you need to know."

"What?"

"Kevin Dunbar is coming up for parole."

Mary's gaze shot to lock with Miriam's as dread seeped into her heart. "What does that mean?"

"If he is granted parole, it means he will be released from prison."

"But they sentenced him to ten years. It's only been four."

"I know, and Nick and I will speak at the hearing and object to his early release, but it may not be enough."

Mary crossed her arms tightly. "Will he come here?"

"He doesn't know where you live. He doesn't know your new name. He doesn't know that I adopted you or that I married Nick. I don't see how he could find you and Hannah."

"He said he would make me pay for speaking against him in court." She bit her lower lip, but it didn't stop the taste of fear that rose in her mouth.

Miriam laid both hands on Mary's shoulders. "He won't find you. Nick and I will see to that. We wanted you to know so it wouldn't come as a shock if he does get an early release, but we don't want you to worry. Here come the men. Why don't you join Hannah in the car?"

"I want to speak to Joshua first. His buggy was crushed and his horse is injured. He has no way to get home. I'm sure Ada won't mind if he comes home with us."

"I'm sure she won't, but it wouldn't be proper for you to offer him a place to stay. You are a single woman. I'm married. I can suggest he stay with my mother."

"But—"

"No buts, Mary. Don't argue about this. An Amish woman is not outspoken. She is modest and humble. You need to cultivate those virtues or you will be perceived as prideful. Don't forget, your actions reflect on Ada, too. Nick spoils you. He's a good man, but he doesn't understand Amish ways."

Mary sighed deeply. Miriam had been raised

Amish and knew what was expected of each member. While Miriam had chosen to live English, Mary had freely chosen the Amish way of life. It wasn't an easy path, but she felt called to follow it. The freedoms she enjoyed by having English parents shouldn't cause her to lose sight of what it meant to live a Plain life. She had placed her life totally in God's hands. She would remain His humble and obedient servant.

Ethan approached them with his chain saw balanced on his shoulder. Miriam said, "Thank you for your assistance, Ethan. Is your family safe?"

"Glad I could help. The storm wasn't bad at our place. I heard about the twister when Clara came home last night from the quilting bee. I went out this morning to see if anyone needed me, or my team. I've cut through a lot of trees blocking lanes and roadways and hauled them aside. I was on my way home when I saw the sheriff's SUV and thought I'd see what he was up to out here."

"I'm glad you did," Nick said as he and Joshua came up beside them.

Mary pinned her gaze to the ground. Joshua must think she was a frightfully forward woman after the way she had acted. "Have you heard if Betsy is safe?" she asked, knowing her friend, whose oldest sister was Ethan's wife, had been headed to the same quilting bee at Katie Sutter's home.

"*Ja*, she is fine. I took Clara and the *kinder* to Wooly Joe's first thing this morning. All the girls were at their grandfather's place. You've never heard such squawking as those sisters do when they have something exciting to talk about. They were getting ready to take food and supplies into Hope Springs."

Mary smiled at him. "I'm glad they're okay. God is *goot*."

"Indeed He is. I need to get my team home. They've had a tough day." Ethan bade everyone farewell and left.

Mary began walking toward Nick's vehicle. She tried not to look back to see if Joshua was watching, but she couldn't help herself. He was.

Joshua watched Mary walk away and a strange sense of loss filled him. This was probably the last time he would see her. He was shocked to realize just how much he wanted to see her again. Under normal circumstances.

Nick laid a hand on Joshua's shoulder. "You must be exhausted."

He tried not to flinch from the man's touch, but it brought back the way the police and the prison guards had grabbed him in the past. "A little," he admitted. His strength was draining away now that the crisis was over.

Miriam glanced toward the car and then turned to him. "Unless you have other plans, why don't you come back to my mother's home with us? You can clean up and have a hot meal, spend the night and then decide what to do in the morning."

As much as he wanted to accept, he didn't want to spend any more time in the sheriff's company. "*Danki*, but I don't think so."

"Suit yourself," Nick said.

Miriam laid a hand on Joshua's arm. "You need a place to stay until you can sort things out and get home. My mother will welcome you. She is Amish, so I know you'll be comfortable there. Not another word—you're coming with us."

She walked away to join Mary and Hannah. Joshua stood rooted to the spot. He hadn't expected this kindness from outsiders. He swallowed hard and hitched a thumb over his shoulder toward the barn. "I have some clothes and a few things in what's left of my buggy that I need. Let me get those and see to my horse."

Nick said, "Leave him tied up here, and I'll have someone bring a trailer and take him to our vet."

"I would appreciate that, if it's not too much trouble." Joshua wasn't sure he had the money to pay for a vet, but his father would send more to cover the bill. Isaac Bowman never skimped on taking care of his animals. It was a lesson he had drilled into his sons.

"No trouble," Nick said. "I've had reports from all over about loose and injured livestock. I have nearly a dozen volunteers with stock trailers helping wherever they are needed and taking all sorts of animals to our vet's clinic. Doc Rodgers has already asked for help from other veterinarians in the state. He'll have someone to look after your horse."

After agreeing to the arrangement, Joshua tethered Oscar where he could reach green grass and water and covered him with a blanket to keep the flies out of the gash. Then he extracted his duffel bag and his few belongings from his crushed buggy and joined Mary's family in the SUV. Hannah greeted him with a big smile. "Bella came back."

Joshua glanced over his shoulder. The Lab mix was in the back of the vehicle panting heavily. "It looks like she had a good run."

"She was chasing a rabbit. She's not supposed to do that," Hannah told him in a low voice.

"Did she catch him?" Joshua asked in a whisper. He shared a smile with Mary, but she quickly looked away.

Hannah shook her head. "She never catches them. She's not very fast. What about your horse?"

"Nick said he'll have someone take him to the vet clinic."

Mary continued to avoid looking at him. He fell silent and remained that way. The sudden change in their circumstances left him feeling tongue-tied and awkward. Or maybe it was because her father kept glancing at him in the rearview mirror. Perhaps going to Mary's home wasn't a good idea.

He hadn't been able to think of a reason to refuse under the sheriff's steely gaze earlier. He didn't want to raise the man's suspicions.

Joshua's parole agreement said he couldn't leave the area without notifying his parole officer. Was he in violation of that even if he was still in the same county? He should have checked before he left home.

The radio crackled and came to life with a woman's voice. "Sheriff, do you read me?"

Nick picked up the mic. "I read you, dispatch."

"We found the missing Keim children. The boys are fine."

Nick grinned at Miriam. "That's great news. Where were they?"

"At their aunt's house. They had gone fishing.

They ran to take cover there when the storm cut them off from home. It took her family a while to dig out afterward and gather their scattered horses and cattle before they brought the kids home."

"That only leaves the McIntyre family unaccounted for."

"Nope, they weren't home. They were out camping in the woods. They came back to town about an hour ago. That's everyone who was unaccounted for, and FEMA is now on scene."

"Good. Let Deputy Medford know. Lance is in charge until I return."

"He already knows, sir."

"Have you had any word on Bishop Zook?"

"He's out of surgery and is expected to make a full recovery."

"The blessings just keep coming. Thanks. I'll be at Ada's house in a few minutes. You can get me on my cell if I don't answer the radio."

"Roger that." The radio went dead.

Joshua glanced at Mary. With her eyes downcast and her hands clasped, she was a lovely sight. Even with the smudges of dirt on her face. Was there anyone special in her life?

He caught sight of Nick watching him in the mirror and looked away, but like a magnetic needle that was always drawn to the north, Joshua's gaze moved back to Mary's face.

He might be attracted to her, but he only had one option where the sheriff's daughter was concerned: go home and forget all about her.

Chapter Five

"Do I have dirt on my face?" Mary didn't look up. She could feel Joshua's gaze on her and wondered what he was thinking. Since entering the car he had been so serious, so worried.

"You do, but I was staring at the destruction out there." He gestured toward the view beyond with his chin.

She looked out the window beside her and gasped. They were driving parallel to the tornado's track. The land bore an enormous scar of destruction. Everywhere the twister had encountered trees, only denuded trunks with stripped and snapped limbs remained. Where the trees had been toppled whole, huge mats of roots stuck in the air. As the storm had passed through wheat fields, it was if an insane harvester had mowed down random sections. Even the grass had been torn out of the pastures, leaving a path of churned dirt in the funnel's wake.

"That's the Keim farm," she said as they rolled past the once neatly tended Amish home. The entire front of the building and the roof was missing. It resembled a dollhouse more than a home. She could see into the rooms of the upper stories, where beds sat covered in bright quilts and clothes still hung on pegs. Below, the stove was all that was left in the remains of the kitchen. Some two dozen Amish men and women were working to clear the rubble. It was one advantage of large Amish families—when someone was in need, there were lots of aunts, uncles and cousins to come help.

Mary pressed her hand to her mouth. "This is so terrible."

Nick said, "It's pretty much the same all the way into Hope Springs. The tornado stayed on the ground for five miles. At times, it was half a mile wide. I've never seen anything like it."

He slowed the SUV and turned in to Ada's lane. The tornado had missed the house by a quarter of a mile. Most of the wind damage was confined to the fields and the crops that had been planted by the young farmer who rented Ada's land. There were shingles missing from the roof of the house and many of Ada's flowers had been blown down.

Nick stopped the vehicle by the front porch, where Ada stood waiting for them. The worry on her face transformed into a bright smile when Mary opened the door and let Hannah out. The child raced up the steps straight into Ada's embrace. Mary followed her.

"I thank *Gott* you are both safe," Ada said as she hugged Mary. "You hadn't been gone more than twenty minutes when the storm hit. When I came outside and saw the twister had gone the same direction you were heading, I dropped to my knees and prayed for you."

"God heard you. He sent Joshua Bowman to help us. You must thank him, as well," Mary replied, turning to introduce her grandmother to him as he got out of her father's vehicle.

Miriam said, "Joshua's buggy was destroyed and his horse was injured. He's a long way from home. I'm hoping you can look after him until he has a chance to sort out what to do next."

Ada raised a hand and beckoned. "Of course. Everyone, please come inside. I've been keeping supper warm in the oven. I must hear what happened to you."

"I can't stay," Nick said. "I have to get back to the command post we have set up in Hope Springs."

"I can't stay, either," Miriam added. "The Red Cross needs volunteers. As a nurse, I know they'll have use for me. I don't know when I'll be back, *Mamm*."

Ada nodded. "I understand."

After another round of hugs from Nick and Miriam, Mary waved goodbye from the porch steps and then led the way into the house. The kitchen smelled of fried chicken and fresh bread. Hannah proceeded to tell her great-grandmother all about their adventure. Ada was shocked and amazed at their narrow escape. Finally, Hannah said, "And then Bella found us. I'm really hungry. Can we eat now?"

Mary laid a hand on her daughter's shoulder. "We should get cleaned up before we sit at the table. Come on. Let's find some decor-free clothes for you." She glanced at Joshua and saw him smile. Pleased by it, she led Hannah away to clean up and change.

When she returned, Joshua was coming in through the front door. He had washed up and changed, as well. His face was clean shaven and his hair was still damp. The house had only one bathroom, so she knew he must have washed at the pump outside. He had a blue plastic basin in one hand.

Joshua offered the basin to Ada. "Thanks for the hot water. It made shaving a whole lot easier."

"*Goot*. You are welcome to stay with us for

as long as you like. I have a spare bed and you won't be any trouble. Now, sit and let me get some food on the table. Mary, slice some bread and fetch a jar of pears from the pantry."

"No pears," Mary and Joshua said together. They shared an embarrassed glance.

Looking confused, Ada said, "I have some peaches if you would rather."

Mary tried not to laugh. "Don't we have some plums?"

"*Ja,* we do."

Mary kissed her grandmother's wrinkled cheek. "Plums will be fine. It's so good to be home."

While Mary and Hannah were busy getting the table set, Ada began pulling pans from the oven. "Joshua, where is your family from?"

"A place called Bowmans Crossing. It's north and west of Berlin. About a day's buggy ride from here."

"I don't know it, but then I've only been in Hope Springs a few years. I moved here from Millersburg. Do you have someone special waiting back home?"

"Not yet."

"So you haven't met the right girl, is that it?"

Mary sent her grandmother a sour glance, but Ada ignored her. Joshua grinned at Hannah.

"I've met her, but she's not quite old enough to marry. I'm going to have to wait a few years."

"He means me, *Mammi*." Hannah put the last plate on the table. "I'm not going to be an old maid."

"At least one of my girls has some sense. What does your family do, Joshua?"

"They farm and run a small business."

"And how did you end up here?"

"He came to look over some property for his father. I think he has answered enough questions for one day." Mary took her place at the table.

"I'm just making conversation and trying to put the poor boy at ease." Ada carried her pan to the table and dished out the creamy potatoes.

When Ada was finished, she took her place at the table and everyone bowed their heads in silent prayer. Because Joshua was the only man at the table, the women waited until he signaled the prayer was finished. Mary hadn't realized how hungry she was until she dug into her grandmother's mouthwatering, crispy fried chicken. It was one of the best meals Mary had ever eaten.

When Joshua was finished, he leaned back in his chair and patted his stomach. "That was mighty *goot*, *danki*."

Ada smiled at him. "It does my heart good to see a man enjoy my cooking. Mary is a fine cook, too."

"I can help clean up," he offered.

Mary and Ada exchanged amused glances. Very few men offered to help with kitchen chores. "I can manage," Ada said. "It would please me if you would read from the Good Book for us when I'm done here."

"It would be my pleasure. Hannah, do you have a Bible story that you like?"

"Noah. I like the story about Noah and all the animals."

Ada smiled. "Very appropriate. As Noah and his family were delivered from a great storm, so were you and your mother. *Gott* is merciful."

Their evenings were often spent with Mary reading passages while Ada caught up with her needlework. It was a pleasant change to have someone else reading to her. Mary listened to the sound of Joshua's voice and realized once again how soothing it was. He had a strong, firm voice. He read with ease and with understanding, pausing occasionally to ask Hannah about something that he had read. She listened intently, seated on the floor in front of him with Bella at her side. He seemed to be a man devoted to his faith, but Mary knew not everyone was what they seemed to be.

When it was time for bed, Ada showed Joshua to the spare room while Mary took Hannah up to her room. She knelt beside Hannah as the child recited her bedtime prayers. Overwhelmed with gratitude for their deliverance, Mary gazed at her child and gave silent thanks. She would never again take moments like this for granted.

Hannah got into bed and pulled the sheet to her chin. "I like this bed much better. It smells *wunderbar.*"

Mary tucked her in. "I agree."

"Will Joshua be here in the morning when I wake up?"

"*Ja*, he will be here."

"I'm glad. I like him. Don't you?"

Mary smiled at her daughter and planted a kiss on her forehead. "I like him, too." Maybe more than she should.

"How old will I have to be before I can marry him?"

Mary bit her lower lip to keep from laughing. "Very old, I'm afraid."

"As old as you?"

Mary chuckled. "At least as old as me."

"Okay. *Guten nacht, Mamm.*"

"Good night and sweet dreams, *liebschen.*" Mary stepped away. Bella took her usual spot on the blue rag rug beside the bed. Mary patted the dog's head. "And sweet dreams for you, too, Bella. You are a very *goot hund.*"

* * *

The following morning, Mary was up bright and early. By the time Ada came out of her room, Mary already had breakfast underway. Although she would have denied it if anyone asked, she wanted to impress Joshua with her cooking skills. Just a little. She pulled a pan of cinnamon rolls from the oven and set it to cool on the counter.

It wasn't long before he came in. "Something smells delicious. I hope it tastes as good as it smells."

"It will. How do you like your eggs?"

"Less than three years old." He tried to pinch off a piece of cinnamon roll, but she batted his hand away.

"Sit down and behave yourself or all you'll get is eggshells."

"Is there coffee?" He glanced hopefully at her.

"In the pot."

He helped himself to a cup and sat at the table. She could feel him watching her. It should have made her nervous, but it didn't. Somehow, it felt comfortable having him in the same room. It shouldn't, but it did, and she wondered why.

What was it about him that made him different from other men? She studied him covertly as she tried to put her finger on it.

His face wasn't particularly handsome, but he

had a strong jaw and a square chin that made him look dependable. She finally decided his eyes were what made him so interesting. They were a soft, expressive brown. They crinkled at the corners when he smiled. She liked that. It proved he smiled often. And he didn't mind being quiet.

Ada and Hannah came in a few minutes later and Mary regretted the loss of her time alone with Joshua.

Did he feel the same? Or was he anxious to leave and get home? Of course he was. Why would he want to spend more time with her?

Ada poured some coffee and leaned her hip against the counter. "We will take food and supplies into Hope Springs when our chores are done. Our neighbors are in need. *Englisch* and Amish alike. We must do what we can."

Mary nodded, ashamed to admit she had forgotten for a little while the tragedy that had struck her community.

They had barely finished breakfast when Bella barked and trotted to the door, wagging her tail. Mary heard the sound of a buggy pulling up outside. Ada rose and went to the window. A bright smile transformed her face as she turned to Mary. "With all that has happened, I clean forgot Delbert Miller was coming by today. I must go out and make him welcome.

Mary, you should come, too." Ada hurried out the front door.

Mary dried her hands slowly on a kitchen towel. "As if I had any choice in the matter."

After the women went out the door, Joshua leaned toward Hannah. "Who is Delbert Miller?"

"*Mammi* says he is the perfect *mann* for *Mamm*. He's going to fix the chicken house roof, but *Mamm* is afraid he'll fall through and squish our chickens."

The perfect man? Joshua rose to his feet and sauntered toward the door to get a look at the paragon.

The buggy in front of the gate was tipped heavily to one side. When the driver got out, Joshua understood the reason. Delbert Miller was a man of considerable size, with a jovial smile and a booming voice to match.

"Good morning, Ada. Good morning, Mary. I see the storm caught you, too."

"Not as bad as some, I hear. What about your place?" Ada asked.

"Not even a branch knocked down."

"You were blessed," Mary said quietly.

"Indeed, I am." Delbert gave Mary a bright smile. His gaze lingered on her face.

Joshua studied Mary closely, looking for her

reaction. To his eyes, she didn't look happy to see the perfect man, and that pleased him.

A team of horses pulling a wagon came up the lane, driven by two young Amish men. The wagon was loaded with lumber.

"Have you brought help?" Ada asked.

Delbert gestured in their direction. "I met Atlee and Moses Beachy on the road. They were on their way home from the Weavers' sawmill with lumber for the town. They insisted on following me in case you needed some repairs."

"That was mighty kind of them, but all I need is a few shingles on the porch roof."

"We have some with us," one of the twins said.

Hannah came outside, but the child stood behind her mother, peeking around the edge of her skirt.

The two young brothers, identical twins, got down from the wagon. "Has anyone seen Hannah Banana?" asked the one who had been driving.

"Could be she got blown away in the big wind," the other one said as they looked around pretending to seek her.

Hannah stepped out from behind Mary. "I almost got blown away. Did you see the tornado? It smashed Joshua's house, and we got stuck in the old cellar. *Mamm* and me and Joshua had to stay there all night. It was full of cobwebs and yucky."

"You don't say?" Delbert looked to Mary for more of an explanation.

Mary, her cheeks glowing pink, gave an abbreviated account to their visitors and introduced Joshua to the men. She sent Hannah back into the house before the little girl could repeat more of the story.

Ada spoke to the twins. "You can get out on the porch roof from the upstairs window. I'll show you. Delbert, I have some cinnamon *kaffi* cake I baked yesterday. Come up to the house when you're finished and have some."

"I'd love to, but it will have to wait. There's a lot of people in need today and the twins and I should get going when we are finished here."

"I understand. Mary will show you what we need done to the chicken *haus*."

Joshua caught Mary's slight hesitation before she nodded. "Come this way."

"Why don't I give you a hand," Joshua offered. He was rewarded with a grateful look from Mary. It appeared that she didn't want to be alone with Delbert.

"I don't reckon I'll need any help." Delbert frowned at Joshua.

"Many hands make quick work," Mary said

brightly. She led the way to the henhouse beside the barn.

The structure had seen better days. There was a hole in the roof where some of the shingles had rotted away. The red paint was faded and peeling from the walls. Joshua suspected a number of boards would need to be replaced. Mary pointed out where the chicken wire around the fenced enclosure was loose and sagging. She opened a gate to the enclosure and stepped back. The black-and-brown hens scurried past her and spread out across the barnyard in search of insects. A large rooster crowed his displeasure, but when all the hens were gone, he followed them and took up a post on the corral fence, where he crowed repeatedly until one of the twins shooed him away.

Delbert turned to Mary. "I'll need a ladder to get up on the roof. Do you have one I can use?"

She pointed toward the barn. "Of course. It's right inside the main door."

Delbert looked disappointed that she didn't offer to show him in person, but he went to fetch it alone.

"I think Hannah might be right," Joshua said, trying to hide a smile.

Mary frowned at him. "About what?"

"She said Delbert was the perfect man for you."

Her eyes narrowed in displeasure. "There's

no such thing as a perfect man. Only God is perfect."

"True enough, but I think you were right about the rest."

"I have no idea what you're talking about."

"If he gets up on the roof of that chicken house, he's going to go right through it."

A reluctant smile tugged at the corner of her pretty mouth. "Why do you think I let all the hens out?"

Delbert returned, carrying the ladder under his arm. He propped it against the building, but before he could climb up, Joshua caught him by the arm. "Why don't you let me go? You and Mary can hand me the supplies I'll need once I am up there."

Delbert looked ready to argue, but thought better of it. "I reckon it would be better for a skinny little fellow like you to test those old boards."

Joshua slapped him on the back. "Exactly what I was thinking. Would you mind if I borrow some of your tools?"

Once he was on the roof of the henhouse, Joshua pried loose the rotted shingles with Delbert's hammer. A section of the plywood roof had to be replaced, but the underlying rafters were sound. Mary handed the new shingles to Delbert, who stood on the ladder and handed them over to Joshua. When Joshua came down, Mary excused herself and went up to the house, leaving the two men alone.

"I can give you a hand restretching the wire fencing," Joshua offered.

"Sure."

Joshua set to work pulling the old staples that held the wire onto the wooden fence posts. "Have you known Mary long?"

"Since she first came here. Four years now, I guess it is."

"Did you know her husband?"

"*Nee*, I'm not sure she was married. If that's the case, I don't hold it against her. We all make mistakes. She's a fine woman, and her little girl is as sweet as they come."

Joshua mulled over that startling bit of information. Did it change the way he felt about her? He wasn't sure, and that shamed him. "Hannah said her father has gone to heaven."

"That is what Mary told Bishop Zook when she joined our congregation. He was an *Englisch* fellow, and that's all I know about him."

Joshua stared at the house. "Does she mourn him still?"

"That I cannot tell you, but she doesn't go to the singings and she has turned down a lot of fellows who have tried to ask her out. Some people say she's too particular. I think she'll come around when the right fellow shows an interest."

Joshua glanced at his companion. "It could be the right fellow doesn't live around here."

Delbert stared at Joshua for a long moment, then he burst out laughing and slapped Joshua on the back hard enough to make him wince. "Only God knows the right one for each of us. If He has someone in mind for her, then that's the one she'll wed, and it won't matter where he's from. We should finish this pen right quick. Others need my help today."

The man had a big heart to match his big frame. "Delbert, I need to find a way to get to Bowmans Crossing as soon as possible."

"Why can't you get home the same way you got here?"

"My buggy was wrecked in the storm and my horse was injured."

"Sorry to hear that. I know a fellow in Hope Springs that drives Amish folks. I'll take you by his house. If he can't take you, well, you're handy with a hammer. You'll be most welcome to join the rest of us in the cleanup."

Joshua was ready to get home. He would miss his growing friendship with Mary, but it was better to leave before the attachment deepened. He had no illusions about his chances with her and the less he had to do with her father, the better. She wasn't the one for him. Joshua didn't believe Delbert was the man for her, either, but he wished the big fellow well in his pursuit of her.

Delbert looked around and lowered his voice. "I should warn you about the Beachy twins."

Joshua looked toward the porch roof, where the two young men were finishing the last of the repairs. "What about them?"

"They have a knack for playing pranks on folks. Harmless pranks for the most part, but beware. You might sit down on a chair and get up to find a red bull's-eye painted on the seat of your pants. It happened to me and I never did figure out how they did it."

Joshua laughed outright at Delbert's pained expression. "I'll beware of them. *Danki.*"

"What can be so funny?" Mary stood at the window watching Delbert and Joshua out by the henhouse.

"What's that, child?" Ada asked. She was at the kitchen table wrapping sandwiches and packing them into boxes.

"Joshua and Delbert are out there slapping each other on the back and laughing like a pair of fools." It was an exaggeration on her part, but she had a sneaking suspicion that they were laughing at her expense.

"The Lord has blessed Delbert with a *wun-*

derbar sense of humor. The man likes to make other people smile. There's nothing wrong in that. Would you pack the plates for me? I expect there will be a lot of hungry people working in Hope Springs today. We'll need to fill some jugs with water, too."

Mary turned away from the window. If the town had seen the same kind of destruction she had witnessed, it would be bad. She was foolish and vain to be worrying about what Joshua Bowman thought of her. She put him out of her mind and began helping Ada prepare lunches.

A few minutes later, Joshua walked in the door. "I wanted to thank you for your hospitality. I'm going to ride into Hope Springs with Delbert and check on my horse, then I'm going to try and find a ride home."

The twins came down the stairs. Atlee patted Hannah on the head. "That should keep the rain from coming in, Hannah Banana. Take care." They doffed their hats and went out.

Joshua went to collect his gear. When he returned, Ada handed him a large box. "Take this with you and tell Delbert to leave it at the Wadler Inn in Hope Springs. The twins said it is still standing. We don't have room for everything in our little cart and our pony Fred can't pull a bigger wagon."

Joshua nodded. "I'll be happy to do that for you. Anything else?"

"*Nee*. Bless you for all your help and for taking care of Mary and Hannah."

"It was my pleasure."

Mary didn't want to say goodbye to him. Not yet. Berlin wasn't that far away. He could find an excuse to return if he wanted to. Did he want to?

"Will we see you again?" she asked quickly, and then looked at her feet. That was too bold of her.

"I would like that," he said quietly.

Her cheeks grew warm. She knew she was blushing. Then she realized he didn't know anything about her. Not really. When he learned her history, he'd run the other way, and that was fine. She didn't need a fellow to like her. Only— wouldn't it be nice if he did?

Hannah ran and bounced to a stop in front of him. "Goodbye, Joshua. When will I see you again?"

"That's hard to say. I live a long way from here."

"But you could come for a visit. He's welcome to visit, isn't he, *Mamm*?"

"Of course he is," Ada said when Mary remained silent.

"*Danki*, Ada. Goodbye, Hannah. Goodbye, Mary."

"Goodbye." Clenching her fingers together until they ached kept Mary from saying anything else. She was a terrible judge of men. The ones she'd thought cared for her had hurt her unbearably. It was better to keep the memory of Joshua's kindness rather than count on him and have him fail her.

When she found the courage to look up, he was already out the door. Her spirits plummeted. Would she ever see him again?

"He was a nice young fellow," Ada said from behind her.

Mary crossed the room to look out the window. "*Ja*, he was."

"I'm gonna miss him," Hannah said and left the room with Bella on her heels.

Mary watched Joshua climb into the buggy with Delbert. The vehicle still tipped heavily to one side. She smiled at the thought of Joshua hanging on to the edge of the seat to keep from sliding into Delbert's lap all the way into Hope Springs. He would make Hannah laugh when he told her the story.

Only he wouldn't be back to share it with her.

And it was better that way. Wasn't it? She didn't want her daughter growing to depend on someone who would let her down.

That was true, but protecting Hannah from disappointment wasn't the whole reason Mary didn't date. The sobering fact was that she didn't want to like someone and then find out he wasn't what he seemed. She was terrified of making another mistake. It was better to depend on God and her family. It was enough. Although she was lonely sometimes.

Mary watched until the buggy was out of sight. She wasn't missing Joshua already, was she? That was ridiculous. They'd known each other for less than two days. A few extraordinary hours. It was foolish to think he'd return to see her and more foolish to wish he would. He surely had a girl waiting back home. He hadn't mentioned one, but it was the Amish way to keep such things private.

He'd been kind to her and to Hannah. It was silly to read anything else into that kindness.

"The Lord provides," Ada said.

Mary shot her grandmother a quick look. "The Lord provides what?"

"All that we need." Ada wore a self-satisfied smile. Humming, she returned to the table to finish packing supplies for their trip into town.

"You're right. He does." Mary joined her grandmother at the table. The Lord had supplied a kind man to come to her rescue in the storm and that was all there was to it. She was grateful, but she wouldn't expect anything more.

Chapter Six

As Joshua rode into town with Delbert, the extent of the destruction became increasingly evident. Where the tornado had reached the town, it had obliterated everything in its path. Houses had been leveled. Mangled cars had been rolled into buildings and trees lay everywhere. Pink insulation and articles of clothing fluttered from the remaining branches of denuded trees that were still upright. It was almost impossible to take in the scope of the damage.

A National Guard soldier had them state their business, and then allowed them to go on after warning them that the town would be closed at 6:00 p.m. and everyone would have to leave unless they were a resident with a habitable house.

A few blocks later, Delbert stopped his horse in front of a building that was little more than a pile of pale bricks. A single wall with an arched window remained standing. The grassy area around the building was covered with brightly colored books.

Delbert whistled through his teeth. "I heard it was bad, but I didn't know it was this bad."

"Was this the library?" Joshua had come to value books in his time behind bars. They'd become a solace during the long days and longer nights in his small cell.

Delbert nodded. "Across the street is the *Englisch* grade school."

That building was in the same condition as the library. A group of women and children were picking up books and papers off the ground and placing them in large blue plastic bins. Up ahead, Ethan Gingerich had his team of draft horses hitched to a fallen tree that had obscured most of a house. At a word from him, the horses leaned into their collars and pulled the massive trunk into the street. A battered white van emerged from the foliage. It had been crushed against the home. An elderly man moved to look it over.

Delbert sighed. "I reckon Samson Carter can't take you to Bowmans Crossing today."

"Why not?"

"Because that is Samson and that is his van. We can ask him if he knows anyone else who can give you a lift if you want?" Delbert waited for Joshua to make a decision.

An elderly woman joined Samson and the two of them stood with their arms around each other surveying the damage to the house and vehicle. She was crying. Everywhere Joshua looked, he saw people picking through the debris of what had once been a town but now resembled an enormous trash heap. Looking down, he noticed an open book on the sidewalk beside the buggy. Its pages fluttered in the breeze. He got out and picked it up. It was a second-grade reader that belonged to a girl named Ann. His mother's name was Anna.

He turned to Delbert. "I reckon I wasn't meant to go home today."

"I thought you had to get back?"

"I have to be home by next Thursday for certain, but my family will understand that I'm needed here until then. I'll write and let them know."

"I'll keep an ear out for anyone going that way."

"I'd appreciate it." Holding the book in his hand, Joshua crossed the street and joined the volunteers at the school.

Mary's eyes brimmed with unshed tears as she made her way past ruined fields and damaged farms to the outskirts of Hope Springs. Ada clutched Hannah close to her side and kept patting the child's back to comfort her. Mary knew her grandmother needed comforting as much as Hannah did. Ada loved the community that had welcomed her wholeheartedly when she first arrived.

Ada had once belonged to a strict, ultraconservative Old Order Amish congregation that didn't allow their young people a choice—they were expected to join the Amish faith. Because their daughter chose to live English, Ada and her husband were forced to shun Miriam. The split was painful for everyone. After Ada's husband died, she knew the only way she could have contact with Miriam was to leave the community she had lived in for sixty years. Hope Springs became a place of healing for both Ada and Miriam, and ultimately for Mary, too.

She loved the community for the same reason—unconditional acceptance from the gentle people who lived devout plain lives amid the rolling farmland and tree-studded hills. Now the village they both loved had been all but destroyed.

The closer they got to town, the more damage they saw. Broken tree limbs and whole uprooted trees blocked the streets and lanes. At the edge of town, houses and businesses were simply gone. Only rubble remained. They heard the sound of chain saws long before they saw the men working to clear debris. Several large vans with brightly painted letters on their sides were lined up along the road. A group of people stood beside them. Long black cables snaked around them and satellite dishes adorned the tops of the vehicles.

Two young men in military uniforms motioned for Mary to stop at the edge of town. Bella lay on the floorboards of the cart with her head on her paws, but she sat up when they stopped.

One soldier approached the cart. "I'm sorry, ladies. We've just been told not to allow anyone down this road. There's a gas leak. Until the utility company can get in to shut it down, it's too dangerous. You'll have to go around."

"We have food for the volunteers. Sheriff Bradley is expecting us," Mary said.

A helicopter buzzed low overhead. Hannah looked up. "What are they doing?"

"They're from one of the television stations. They're taking video of the storm damage."

Hannah gave him a puzzled look. "What's a video?"

He smiled. "Pictures for television."

"Why?"

"Because this is news." He pointed toward a

side street. "The command post has been set up at the Wadler Inn. If you go two blocks west, you might be able to go north from there. There are still a lot of downed trees and power lines, but I think you can get your buggy through. The power is off to the whole town, so don't worry about touching the lines. Just be careful."

"We will. *Danki*." Mary started to turn Fred and head the way the young soldier had indicated. The group from the news van approached. One of them carried a large camera on his shoulder aimed in their direction. They were blocking Mary's way. A woman in a bright red dress came to the side of the cart and held a microphone toward Mary. "Vanetta Jones of WWYT News. Can you tell us how the Amish community is reacting to this disaster?"

The pony, frightened by the commotion, shied away. Mary had trouble controlling him. "We're here to help our neighbors however we can."

Ada turned her face away from the camera and held up her hand. "Please, no pictures." Mary struggled to control the pony, who was threatening to bolt. "Please, let us pass."

The cameraman and reporter stepped aside. Mary urged her pony forward, happy to leave the intrusive people behind her.

"I can't believe this is the same town," Ada

said quietly. "I don't recognize it. I'm not sure which street we're on."

Mary wasn't, either. Nothing identifiable remained among the piles of debris. A sea of broken tree limbs blocked her way. Crushed cars were scattered helter-skelter among roofless and wrecked homes with large red *X*s painted on them. Halfway down the second block, an English family sat huddled together on concrete steps. A mother and father with three children, one a baby in the mother's arms. The baby was crying. The whole family wore dazed expressions. Their clothes were dirty, and only two of them had shoes on. A damaged van sat nearby. The house the steps once led up to was completely gone. Only the bare floors remained. All the nearby homes were in a similar state.

Mary stopped the buggy, handed the reins to Ada and got out. Although she was leery of strangers, she couldn't pass by these people in need. She pulled a box from the stack behind her seat and carried it to the young couple.

"We have some food and some water for you."

The man took the box. "Thank you. I don't know you, do I?"

"We've never met. Do you have somewhere to go?"

"We slept in our van last night but it doesn't run. We can't leave."

Mary's heart ached for them. "We're on our way to the inn. If they have room, I'll send word."

"We don't have the money to stay there. I don't know where my wallet is." He looked around as if expecting to see it on the ground.

"You won't need money," Ada said quickly. "God commands us to care for one another. There won't be any charge."

Bella hopped out of the cart and trotted up to the young boy and girl seated beside the man. Hannah followed her. The big dog sat and offered her paw to shake. The boy tentatively reached for her foot and shook it. He was rewarded with a quick lick on the cheek.

Hannah said, "This is my dog, Bella. She's sorry your house got blowed away." All the children began to pet her. Their faces slowly lost their hollow expressions.

Mary spoke to the young mother. "What do you need for the baby?"

She glanced around. "Everything. Diapers, formula, a crib."

"All right. We'll be back later. For now, I have some dry blankets and some kitchen towels you can use as cloth diapers until we return." Mary got the supplies from the back of the cart and gave them to her.

"Bless you." The young mother started crying and her husband pulled her close.

"Hannah, come on." Mary held out her hand.

"Can we help them look for their cat, *Mamm*? It ran away in the storm."

"We'll worry about Socks later," the father said to his children.

"There is an animal collection station being set up at the vet clinic north of town. Your cat may be there. If it is, someone will look after it until you claim it," Mary said.

The father gave her a tired smile. "Thanks. That's one less worry."

Mary returned to the cart and lifted Hannah onto the seat. Bella jumped in and lay down on the floorboards again. Ada kept the reins and clicked her tongue to get Fred moving.

They made their way toward the Wadler Inn, leaving the street in a few locations and traveling over people's lawns to get past downed trees. When they arrived at their destination, they witnessed a beehive of activity. Buggies and carts were lined up along the street next to pickups and cars. Amish and English worked side by side carrying in supplies and donations. A large Red Cross tent was being set up down the street at the town's small park. From here, it was easy to see most of the town remained intact, but the tornado had cut a path through the southwest end with merciless ferocity.

An Amish boy about ten years old ran up to the cart. "I'll take care of your pony if you're staying a spell." He pointed toward the outskirts of town. "We're putting them in Daniel Hershberger's corral."

"*Danki.* How did your family fare?"

"We didn't have much damage. Just a few trees down, nothing like here. God was good to us."

"Something good will come from all of this, too," Ada said, stepping down and handing him the reins. "Troubles are God's way of getting our attention. They remind us that this world is not our eternal home and our time here is not our eternal life. Tie the pony to the hitching rail, but leave him harnessed to our cart for now. We'll need him to bring another family here."

"Okay." The boy did as she instructed, then crossed the street to where another Amish buggy had pulled up in front of the hardware store.

Inside the lobby of the inn, Mary and Ada found Emma Yoder and her mother, Naomi Shetler, directing the placement of supplies and sending tired first responders and volunteers up to the guest rooms for a few hours of rest. Both women looked exhausted. Emma owned and operated the inn with her husband, Adam.

Naomi had worked at the inn for years until her marriage to Wooly Joe Shetler, a reclusive sheep farmer and Betsy Barkman's grandfather.

Ada greeted each of them and said, "What can we do to help? We've brought water, sandwiches, cakes and extra bedding. Who needs to be fed?"

Emma swept a few stray hairs back from her forehead. "Bless you. Take the food around to the café entrance. Betsy and Lizzie are preparing lunches there. Give the bedding to Katie and Nettie. They're upstairs. We had forty souls sleeping on the floor in here last night. There won't be that many tonight. A lot of folks have relatives who are taking them in, but we will still have some with nowhere to go."

"Have you room for a family of five?" Mary asked. "We passed them on our way here."

Emma gave her a tired smile. "We'll make room."

"They have a newborn baby."

"I'll have Adam bring our son's cradle down from the attic. Where is that man?" She turned and went in search of him.

Mary caught sight of Betsy coming in from the café. When Betsy saw her, she raced across the room and threw her arms around Mary. "I'm so glad you're okay. You can't know how worried I was when I heard your empty buggy had been found. I didn't know you were safe until late last night when Ethan brought us word."

"It was quite an adventure. I'll have to tell you about it when we have the time."

Betsy nodded. "That may be a while."

She turned toward Naomi behind the front desk. "I've got six dozen cookies and sandwiches made along with three gallons of tea and lemonade. Shall I take it to the Red Cross tent or will we be serving people here?"

"Go check with the Red Cross and see what they want us to do. We'll be happy to serve people here if they need us to. Hannah, I know you'd like to see your friends. The Sutter *kinder* are upstairs with their mother helping fold linens and sorting donations. Would you like to join them?"

Hannah looked to Mary. "May I?"

"*Ja*, but I don't want you going outside. There is too much going on and too many things you could get hurt on."

"Okay." She darted up the stairs as fast as she could.

Ada and Mary went outside and brought in their contributions. After giving them to Naomi, Mary turned to Ada. "I'm going to go back and pick up that family."

Ada nodded. "*Goot*. I will see what I can do here."

Mary returned to the cart and retraced her way to the family without a home. They were still sitting on the steps, but the baby wasn't crying. She stopped the pony on their lawn. "There is room for you at the inn. I can take you there now."

The husband shook his head. "We can't take your charity. We will manage."

"How?" his wife asked.

He scowled at her. "I can take care of this family."

"Please," Mary said. "We have a place for you to stay, but we are in need of many hands to help. It will not be charity. We will put you to work."

"This is very kind of you," the young mother said as she got up from the stoop. She handed the baby to Mary, got in and took the baby back. The father sighed and followed. He loaded the two older children in the rear of the cart and climbed up beside his wife.

When they arrived back at the inn, Mary turned the young family over to Emma's capable hands and went to the kitchen. Betsy was back from the Red Cross tent. She was packing sandwiches into a large box. "We are going to take half of these to the other end of the park and set up there. I'll take this basket. You grab a box and come with me. I can't wait another minute to hear about your adventure."

The two women walked side by side down the street and across the park. Mary gave Betsy a carefully edited version of her time with Joshua. Although she thought she had done a good job of downplaying the incident, Betsy wasn't satisfied.

"Tell me more about this young man. Wasn't it scary to be alone with a stranger?"

"I wasn't alone. I had Hannah with me. I was thinking about her, and about how to make things less frightening for her. He was, too. I wasn't thinking about myself."

Betsy peeked at Mary through lowered lashes. "Was he nice-looking?"

"I suppose he was. He was kind. That matters more than looks." He had been kind. And funny. And good with Hannah. All the things she dreamed a man should be. He had appeared in time to save them and now he was gone. She'd likely never see him again. She knew it was probably for the best, but it didn't feel that way.

"It's too bad that he left before I had the chance to thank him for taking care of my very best friend and her daughter."

Just then, Mary caught sight of Nick and Miriam. They were speaking to the woman in the red dress who had tried to interview her. Betsy said, "I heard that we made the national news."

"What a sad way for our town to become famous. They tried to interview Ada and me on our way into town."

"Did they? We'll have to find somewhere to watch the news. Maybe you'll be on it."

"We can't watch TV even if we wanted to."

"No one from the church will object if we happened to see it at an *Englisch* friend's home. Who has a television? The hardware store has one they keep on in the back."

"No one in town has electricity, Betsy. The power is out."

Betsey giggled. "That's right. I forgot. We're just used to being without it, so I didn't notice. I'm sure they'll have generators running soon. The *Englisch* can't do much without electricity."

Mary saw several members from her church setting up benches and tables. "I think that's where we're supposed to be."

She put her box on the nearest table. Betsy opened her basket and began setting out plates and a platter of cookies. Mary began unpacking the sandwiches and piling them on a plastic tray.

"I didn't think we would meet again so soon."

Mary looked up in astonishment. Joshua stood in front of her with a plate in his hand. "Joshua! What are you still doing here? I thought you were going home?" Her heart began fluttering like a wild bird in her chest.

"Delbert took me to Samson Carter's place, but his van is out of commission. It had a rather large tree on top of it. When I saw how much work needed to be done here, I thought I might as well stay for a few days longer. I dropped a note to my family in the mail so they won't worry about me. Happily, the post office is in one piece."

Flushing with pleasure at seeing him again, Mary continued setting out the sandwiches. "That's very kind of you to stay."

"Are you Mary's mystery man?" Betsy regarded him across the table.

"I'm not much of a mystery." He reached for a sandwich and a couple of cookies.

"Betsy, this is Joshua Bowman. Joshua, this is my friend Betsy Barkman." It was silly, but it felt odd introducing him to her friend as if he were an old acquaintance. They barely knew each other.

"I'm grateful you were able to rescue Mary and Hannah. I'm so glad I have a chance to tell you that. Oh, I see Alvin over there. I need to find out how his mother is doing. She was knocked down when a tree branch slid off the roof of a house and hit her this morning."

Betsy hurried away, but looked back with a

wink for Mary before catching up with Alvin. The two of them had been dating for several years, although Betsy said she wasn't sure he was the one.

"This must be hard for you," Joshua said.

Mary ducked her head. How could he possibly know how confused and excited she felt when he was near? "Why would seeing you again be hard for me?"

"I meant it must be hard for you to see your community in ruins."

She felt like a fool. "It is sad, but look how everyone is working together. Friends are helping friends. Strangers are helping strangers. It will take a lot of work, but we'll get through this."

"I was wondering if your grandmother's offer of a place to stay was still open? If not, I'm sure I can find another family to put me up."

"Ada and Hannah will be happy to have you stay."

"And you, Mary? Will you be happy if I do?" His voice was low enough that only she could hear him.

She quickly looked down. She was excited at the prospect, but it also gave her pause. She already liked him too much. Her track record with liking and trusting the wrong men made her leery of repeating those mistakes. She chanced a glance in his direction. He was watching her with a small grin on his face that set butterflies loose in her midsection. She was trying to think how she should answer him when a group of volunteers arrived and began helping themselves to the food. Joshua moved aside. Maybe she should pretend she hadn't heard his question.

Someone called his name. Mary saw Ethan Gingerich gesturing to him from the back of a wagon. Joshua waved to acknowledge him.

Looking at Mary, he tipped his head toward Ethan. "I need to get back to work."

"But you haven't finished your lunch."

"I'll take it with me."

She tried for an offhand tone to make it seem as if she didn't care where he stayed. "Our cart is at the Wadler Inn. You can find us there when you're ready to call it a day. Unless you find someplace else you'd rather stay."

Joshua tempered his disappointment. He could hardly expect Mary to be overjoyed about spending more time with him. He was little more than a stranger, but at least she hadn't rescinded the invitation. That was something.

He wasn't sure what it was about Mary, but he was drawn to her in a way he had never been drawn to another woman. Maybe it was the circumstances of their first meeting. Maybe when their lives weren't hanging in the balance and the world wasn't smashed beyond recognition he would be able to see her in an ordinary light and this strange attraction would fade.

Or maybe she would always be special in his eyes.

For now, he was happy he hadn't been able to return home today. Seeing her again made the whole day brighter.

He glanced toward the command tent and found Sheriff Bradley watching him. A chill settled between Joshua's shoulder blades. If her father learned of his record, Joshua could kiss his chances of spending time with Mary good-bye. And maybe even his freedom.

Was he being a fool to risk it?

Chapter Seven

Joshua caught sight of Mary several times during the day while he avoided being anyplace near where the sheriff happened to be working. Like many of the women, Mary manned the food stations and helped wherever she was needed. More than once, he saw her loading smashed lumber, chunks of insulation and broken Sheetrock into the waiting trucks lined up along Main Street. Late in the afternoon, he saw her with her arms full of dirty toys as she carried them toward the lost-and-found area. She worked tirelessly, as did most of the residents and volunteers who had flooded in to help the devastated town.

After a long, hard day of sorting books, cutting up trees and clearing the streets of debris so that vehicles could get through, Joshua was bone tired when he arrived at the inn for a ride to Mary's house. He found her sorting through papers and photographs that had been brought in by the volunteers. She looked up and caught sight of him. A smile brightened her face before it quickly became blank. She looked down and resumed her work.

Every time he thought she was glad to see him, she retreated just as quickly.

He crossed the lobby, stepping around people rolled up in blankets and sleeping bags. He spied Ada sitting in a large wing-back chair by the fireplace. She was asleep. Bella lay quietly beside her. He didn't see Hannah. When he reached Mary, he spoke quietly so as not to disturb the people trying to rest. "They told us to go home. The National Guard is locking down the town for the night soon. No one's going to be allowed in after curfew. They are asking only residents to stay."

"All right." Mary brushed the back of her hand across her forehead. "The rest of this can wait. I'm sure there will be more by morning. A woman from New Philadelphia brought in a photo album and a checkbook. She said she found them in her rosebushes. That's thirty miles from here. The checkbook belongs to Bishop Zook, but no one here knows who the photograph album belongs to."

"There are so many people trying to protect

what is left of their homes that they haven't had time to search for missing items. We must have covered fifteen damaged houses with tarps this afternoon alone. Have you heard any more about your bishop's condition?"

"He's in intensive care, but he's improving. One of his ribs punctured his spleen."

"I'm sorry. Let us hope God speeds his healing. If you want to keep working, I'll find a place to wait until the Guard makes us leave."

She shook her head. "Let me tell Emma and Miriam that we're going."

He looked around. "Where is Hannah?"

"She is out back with Katie and her little ones. I'll go get her and then wake Ada."

"Does she know I'm coming home with you?"

"I told her you might. I wish we could let her nap a little while longer. I'm afraid she did too much today."

"Maybe you can convince her to stay home with Hannah tomorrow."

"I'll try. Sometimes convincing Ada to do something that's for her own good can require delicate maneuvering."

He chuckled. "It must run in the family."

She rolled her eyes. "If you want to be helpful, go outside and find the boy who stabled our pony."

"Consider it done."

Joshua found a pair of boys sitting on the curb. One of them knew which pony belonged to Ada. He left at a run and returned a few minutes later with Fred. Joshua had the pony harnessed to the cart by the time Mary came out. He helped Ada up onto the seat. She was almost too tired to make it.

"*Danki*, Joshua. These old bones don't work as well as they used to. I'm glad you chose to stay with us."

He helped Mary up next, lifted Hannah up to her and then climbed in himself. Bella wanted on the floorboard but he made her get in back. It was a tight squeeze with all of them on the bench seat, but he didn't mind being pressed close to Mary. There was something comforting about her presence.

As he drove out of town, he was forced to stop as a police officer directed some heavy equipment across the road. A news van sat beside them on the shoulder of the road. The reporter, a man with gray hair, was speaking to the camera. "As you can see behind me, Amish families like this one have poured in to help this community in horse-drawn wagons, buggies and carts. Although very few Amish live in this town of two thousand people, it hasn't made any difference to them. Helping their neighbor goes far beyond the confines of religion and town limits."

Joshua ignored the camera that swung to include them. Mary and Ada turned their faces away. Hannah looked around him and waved. A woman behind the cameraman waved back. When the heavy equipment was safely over the road, they were allowed to go.

Something the reporter said stuck in Joshua's mind as he urged Fred into a trot down the highway. Joshua glanced at Mary and Hannah sitting beside him. The man had thought they looked like a family.

It was growing dark by the time they finally reached home. Hannah had fallen asleep in Mary's arms several miles back. Now her arm was numb from holding her daughter. Ada got down and headed for the house with lagging steps. Bella hopped out and loped toward the barn. Joshua noticed that Mary was having trouble.

"Here, let me take her." He lifted Hannah off her lap.

Mary rubbed some feeling back into her arm. "She's getting heavy. I don't know how she has grown up so quickly."

"My mother used to threaten to tie a brick on top of my hat so I wouldn't grow so fast." Joshua settled Hannah over his shoulder and extended a hand to help Mary down from the cart.

"Did it work? Maybe I'll try it."

"It didn't work for any of her sons."

Mary hesitated to take his hand, but her common sense won out. He was just being kind. She had to keep reminding herself of that. She allowed him to help her down and then quickly stepped away from him, still rubbing her tingling arm. She reached for Hannah, but Joshua shook his head.

"I'll take her to bed if you'll show me the way."

"All right." She walked up to the house and held the door for him.

Ada was unpacking the baskets they had taken into town. Mary said, "Leave them, Ada. I'll take care of them as soon as I get Hannah into bed."

"*Danki*, child. I don't know why I'm so tired."

"It was an emotionally difficult day," Joshua said.

"It was. *Guten nacht*, all." Ada walked down the hall to her bedroom at the rear of the house.

Mary led Joshua up the narrow staircase to the second floor. She opened the door to Hannah's room and turned on the battery-operated lamp she kept on Hannah's bedside table. Joshua laid Hannah gently on her bed and stepped back.

He treated her daughter with such tenderness. If nothing else about him appealed to her that would. The trouble was *everything* about him pleased her.

Mary removed Hannah's prayer *kapp* and shoes and quickly changed her into her nightgown without waking her. Joshua crossed to the window and opened it to let in the cool night air as Mary tucked the sheets around Hannah and kissed her forehead.

"She's a sweet child," he said softly.

"She is the sun and the stars."

They left the room together. Mary closed the door quietly. Then it was just the two of them in the dark hall. His nearness sent a tingle of awareness across her skin like a soft evening breeze. He smelled of wood shavings and his own unique scent that she remembered from their time together in the cellar. She stepped back and crossed her arms. "I hope you are comfortable in the spare room."

"Compared to the backseat of my buggy and the chairs we tried to sleep in night before last, the spare bed felt *wunderbar.*"

"Was it only two days ago? It seems like ages." She began walking down the stairs.

"A lot has happened since then. I got to meet Delbert."

Mary tried to smother her smile but it broke free, anyway. "Was the ride with him comfortable?"

"I wouldn't say it was comfortable. My arm

was mighty tired of hanging on to the edge of the seat by the time we reached town."

"Delbert is a good man. I shouldn't make fun of him."

"He's a hard worker. Not fast, but he gets the job done."

Crossing to the stove, she stoked the coals and placed a kettle over the back burner when the embers flared to life. Although the *Ordnung* of their church allowed propane stoves, Ada refused to get rid of her wood-burning one.

"Would you like some tea?" Mary wanted to prolong their time together. She shouldn't. She should go to bed and forget he was even in the house.

Like that's going to happen.

"I would love some tea. *Danki.*" He took a seat at the table.

Suddenly nervous, Mary finished unpacking the baskets, making a mental list of the things she would need to take with her in the morning. After putting out a pair of white mugs, she placed a tea bag in each one. She could feel Joshua's gaze on her as she moved around the kitchen. He didn't speak. Thankfully, the kettle began to whistle. She took it from the stove and filled the waiting mugs.

She carried them to the table and handed

him one. "I would've thought you could have found a ride to Berlin with some of the *Englisch* volunteers."

"I did think of that, but by then I had seen the extent of the destruction and I wanted to help. I can stay a few days. The vet told me Oscar won't be fit to travel for at least a week unless I have him trailered home. You wouldn't believe the number of injured horses and cattle that have been brought in. To say nothing of the dogs and cats."

"So you're staying for a week?" A flicker of excitement shimmered through her.

"Oh, I don't have to stay here for that long. I can find somewhere else."

Don't make it seem important.

"I reckon the chair in your great-uncle's basement is still available."

Joshua chuckled. "As a last resort, I'll keep that in mind."

Mary took a sip of her tea. "You can stay with us. Ada won't mind and Hannah will love having you. I can ask Nick to have Oscar brought here. We can look after him for you. We have room in the barn. It's the least we can do."

"That would be great. I'll pay you for his keep."

"There are plenty of chores you can do. The

corncribs are going to have to be rebuilt before fall."

"I'll see what I can do after I get back from
Hope Springs tomorrow."

Mary sighed deeply. "This is not what I imagined I'd be doing a week ago."

"What do you mean?"

"Sorting through the wreckage of people's
homes and lives, looking for something to salvage for them."

"It's not something anyone imagined. It's just
what needs to be done."

"You sound very practical."

"Do I? My family often accuses me of being
the dreamer. The fellow who always thinks he
can make things better, help people change."

"Do I detect a hint of bitterness?"

He dunked his tea bag up and down without
looking at her. "Sometimes people don't want
to change."

"Sometimes they don't know how," she said
gently.

"He knows how. He just won't."

"Someone in your family?"

Joshua shook his head. "I don't want to bore
you with our problems."

"You saved my life. Feel free to bore me.
Sometimes talking helps."

He hesitated, then said, "I have a brother who left."

"Left the Amish?"

Joshua hunched over his cup, staring at it intently. "*Ja.* Luke got in with bad company. He got into drugs."

"It happens." She rubbed the scar on her wrist. Her past was checkered with bad company and all the trouble it had brought her. Hannah was the only good thing to come out of that horrible time.

Joshua sat back. "*Nee*, Mary, it doesn't just happen. My brother made a choice. He hurt a lot of people."

"Including you?"

"Including me and everyone in our family."

"I'm sure he regrets that."

Joshua sneered. "Not that I can see."

"Where is he now?"

"Far away."

He looked so sad. She wanted to reach out and comfort him, but she held back. "I'm sorry."

"*Danki*, but it doesn't matter. He is my brother and I love him, but he is lost to us."

"Perhaps not. With God, all things are possible. I'll pray for him."

"You are a good woman, Mary."

The look he gave her warmed her all the way through. She basked in the glow of his compliment. When had she started needing someone's praise?

When he started giving it. When he called her brave outside the cellar.

Had it only been yesterday morning? It seemed as if she had known him for years.

He took a sip of tea. "Tell me how you ended up being adopted by two *Englisch* people? That's got to be unusual for an Amish girl."

She came back to reality with a thud. When he learned about her past, he would know she wasn't good and she wasn't brave. She took one last sip of her tea and carried the mug to the sink. "It's a long story. I think I will save it for some evening when I'm not so tired."

"Sure. I understand."

She left him sitting at the table and went to her room, but it was a long time before she fell asleep.

Someone was patting his face. Joshua cracked one eyelid. Hannah was bending close.

"Are you awake?" she whispered.

"Maybe." He glanced toward the bedroom windows. Only a faint pink color stained the eastern horizon.

"*Mamm* said I wasn't to bother you until you were awake."

He sat up stiffly and rubbed his face with both hands. "Okay. I'm awake. What do you need?"

"The wagon has a broken wheel."

Did they have a wagon as well as a cart? He didn't remember seeing one. How did a wheel get broken at this hour? "Do you mean the cart has a broken wheel?"

"*Nee*, my wagon does." She shoved a wooden toy in front of his face.

He took it from her and held it out where he could focus on it. The rear axle was broken and the right rear wheel was split in half. "This looks bad."

She held her hands wide. "I know. I can't take my chickens to market without it."

He heard the faint clatter of pans in the kitchen downstairs. Was Mary up already? He sighed heavily. He'd gotten out of the habit of rising early when he was in prison. There was no point. He stared at the broken toy. "How did this happen?"

Hannah spun to glare at Bella, sitting quietly behind her. "She got in it and she was too big."

The Lab perked up and wagged her tail happily.

The image of the eighty-pound dog trying to fit in a toy wagon that was only ten inches wide made Joshua look closely at Hannah. Something wasn't right. "Are you sure that's how this happened?"

Hannah stared at her bare feet. "I wanted her to get in, but she wouldn't. So I showed her how to jump in and the wheel broke."

"You jumped in the wagon?"

"Only because Bella wouldn't do it."

"I think the results would have been the same either way, but it's not right to blame Bella for something you did."

"I know. But can you fix it? *Mamm* says she can't."

He could if he was home and in his father's workshop. He didn't have the tools he would need to fashion the parts here. He hated to admit he couldn't help so he tried a different approach. "I'm afraid we'll have to take it to a wheelwright. Is there a buggy maker in these parts?"

"Levi Beachy makes buggies in Hope Springs."

"If his business hasn't blown away, I'll take your wagon in and see what he can do. It needs a new axle as well as a wheel. But Hannah, a lot of folks need their wagons and buggies repaired, too. Ones that aren't toys. It might take a while for it to get fixed."

"Okay. I guess I'll take my chickens to market next week."

"I'm sorry I couldn't be more help."

She picked up a cardboard box with paper cut-outs of chickens in it and headed to the kitchen. "That's okay. *Mamm*, Joshua is awake!"

Mary peeked around the door frame. He managed a little wave. She gave her daughter the same look Hannah had turned on Bella. "Did you wake him up?"

"Bella did."

He couldn't let that slide. "Hannah, what did I tell you?"

Her little shoulders slumped. "That it's not right to blame Bella for things I do."

Mary frowned. "So you did wake him."

"Only because Bella wouldn't do it. Do I have to go to the corner in the kitchen now?"

"*Ja*, right this minute." Mary pointed toward the stairs. Bella followed Hannah with her head down and her tail between her legs.

Mary dried her hands on her apron. "I'm sorry, Joshua. You can go back to sleep for a while. She won't bother you again."

"I'm awake. I might as well see what can be salvaged of your corncribs after I take care of the horses."

"All right. Would you feed the chickens and the cow, too, while you are out there?"

"Sure. Do you want me to milk the cow?"

"Ada will milk her. They get along. She likes to kick everyone else."

"Ada does?"

Mary giggled. He adored the sound. "*Nee*, Rosie the cow does."

"Then I'll leave milking Rosie to Ada."

Mary turned around and left. Scratching his head and yawning, he headed for the bathroom. If he kept moving, he'd wake up. Every muscle in his body ached. It had been months since he'd done as much physical labor as he'd done yesterday, and it showed.

Twenty minutes later, he was wide-awake and pitching hay from the open door of the barn loft down to the horse, the pony and a doe-eyed brown-and-white Guernsey cow. His stiff muscles were loosening up and the fog had lifted from his brain. A decent night's sleep could do wonders for a man. As could walking outside without seeing high barbed-wire fences and guard towers.

He had stayed up late last night writing a letter to his parents. He wanted to share his thoughts, and he knew it would ease his mother's mind to hear more from him. It had been hard to describe the damage he saw and how the lives of people had been altered in Hope Springs, but it had been easy to write about Mary, Ada and Hannah. He might have written too much about Mary, but everything seemed to revolve around her.

He drew a deep breath as he leaned on his pitchfork and watched dawn break over the land. The springtime air was fresh and crisp. Thick dew covered the grass and sparkled where the sunlight touched it. If he faced south from the hayloft door, he could see fields of young corn just a few inches tall. By late summer, it would be higher than a man's head and by winter it would be stacked in rows of shocks waiting to feed the cattle. It was good land. A man could make a fine living for his family farming it. At the moment, it was green and brimming with the promise of new life.

"Joshua, breakfast is ready," Mary called from the front porch.

"Coming." He tossed one more forkful of hay to the animals and went down the hayloft ladder. When he came out of the barn, he saw the sheriff's white SUV coming up the lane.

Joshua's joy in the morning vanished as dread seeped in to replace it. The one thing he hadn't included in his letter was Mary's relationship to an Englisch lawman.

The vehicle rolled to a stop in front of the house. The passenger-side door opened and Miriam stepped out with a friendly smile on her face. "Good morning, Joshua. I thought you would have been well on your way home by now."

Nick got out, too. His smile wasn't near as friendly. Joshua fixed his gaze on the ground. "I thought I would stay for a few days and help with the cleanup."

"All help is appreciated," Nick said. He and Miriam both looked weary.

She sighed deeply. "Yes, it is, and sorely needed. I don't know how the town will ever recover from this."

Joshua couldn't think of anything to say. Fortunately, Hannah came flying out of the house just then. "Papa Nick, can you fix my wagon?"

He scooped her up in his arms. "What happened to your wagon?"

"Bella—" Hannah glanced at Joshua and lowered her face. "I mean—I jumped in it and it broke. Bella didn't do it."

"You are just in time to eat," Ada said from the doorway. "Come in."

"I was hoping you'd ask." Nick set Hannah on the ground and they all went toward the house.

Joshua followed slowly.

Breakfast was a feast. Mary had prepared bacon and scrambled eggs. There were fresh hot biscuits with butter and honey and oatmeal with brown sugar and cinnamon. He picked at his food. It was hard to have an appetite when he was seated beside the sheriff. Every bruise, every humiliation Joshua had suffered during his arrest and time in prison came back to choke him. He rubbed his wrists at the memory of handcuffs chafing his flesh. Bile rose in his throat.

Ada poured coffee into the cup in front of him, bringing him back to the present. A rich, enticing aroma rose from the steaming liquid. He grasped the cup and raised it to his lips. It was hot, but the slightly bitter brew settled the nausea in his stomach. He looked up to thank her and noticed that she still had dark circles under her eyes.

Nick seemed to have noticed, as well. "Miriam and I'll head into town after we're done with breakfast. Ada, you and Mary don't need to come in today. There will be plenty of volunteers to help."

"I think I will remain here. I've gotten behind on my own work." Ada sat down at the table.

Hannah popped up. "Can I go to town with you, Papa Nick?"

"Nee." Mary shook her head. "Papa Nick has too much to do to look after you in all that chaos. Besides, I need you to stay home and help *Mammi*."

"But how will I get my wagon fixed?"

"I'll see to it," Joshua assured her. She seemed content with that.

Miriam laid a hand on Mary's sleeve. "Are you going back today?"

"I am. Betsy and I have signed up for shifts at the food station."

"You can ride with us," Nick offered.

"That's all right. I know you need to get going, and I'm not ready. Joshua and I will take the cart."

Nick sent Joshua a sharp glance. "As long as you are both careful. The place is a zoo."

"We will be," Mary assured him. Joshua kept his gaze on his half-eaten eggs.

"May I have another biscuit? How long are you staying, Joshua?" Nick asked.

"I have to be home by Thursday so I need to leave by Wednesday."

Mary passed the plate of biscuits to Nick. "Can you have Joshua's horse brought here? We can look after him, and that will free up space at the vet clinic."

"Sure. I'll see to it. Will you be staying here, Joshua?"

He couldn't tell from Nick's tone what he thought about the idea. He glanced at Mary to gauge her reaction. She kept her eyes downcast. Joshua cleared his throat. "Yes, if it's not too much trouble for Ada and Mary."

"It's no trouble," Ada declared. "I'll put you to

work. I need wood cut for the stove. I need my corncribs fixed. I have plenty to keep you busy."

Nick nodded slowly, but didn't say anything. Joshua had the impression he wasn't pleased, but there was little he could do about it.

Joshua shifted uneasily in his chair and took another sip of coffee. Had the sheriff noticed his nervous attitude? Hopefully he hadn't, but something in the man's intense gaze made Joshua doubt he missed much.

The sheriff and Miriam left shortly after that, much to Joshua's relief. Later, as he waited beside the cart for Mary to join him, his spirits rose with a growing sense of anticipation. The ride would only take thirty minutes or so, but it would give him thirty minutes alone with Mary, and he liked that idea.

That became the pattern for the next several days. Joshua took care of the animals in the mornings, then headed to breakfast, where Nick and Miriam joined them at Ada's insistence. She wanted to be kept apprised of the progress and needs in the community and she said no one was better informed than Nick. Miriam was able to pass along updates on Bishop Zook and the other injured people. Joshua strongly suspected part of Ada's plan was to insure her daughter was getting enough food and rest and not working herself into the ground.

After breakfast, Joshua would drive Mary into Hope Springs. They would go their separate ways in town, but they often found each other for a quiet lunch in the park. The work was exhausting and sad, but nearly everyone worked to keep each other's spirits up. One afternoon, an impromptu singing took place when five teenage Amish girls began a hymn in the park. They were soon joined by a group of young men, and for thirty minutes the cares of the volunteers and townspeople were lifted away by the sweet voices of the a cappella group.

In the evenings, Joshua rebuilt Ada's corncribs and read from the Bible after supper. Once Ada went to bed, he and Mary talked about their day over a mug of tea at the kitchen table. When he was alone in his room, he wrote to his family each night. He found himself writing more about Mary and Hannah than about the storm damage and recovery.

As he sealed the envelope of his current letter, he stared at it and wondered what his family would make of Mary if they met. Would they like her as much as he did? Would they approve of her adoptive parents?

He sighed as he realized he could easily go

home now. There were plenty of helpers in Hope Springs, but he didn't want to leave.

Not just yet.

Chapter Eight

~~~

Mary sat down on the cart seat beside Joshua on Saturday morning and worked hard to control her nervousness. It was another simple wagon ride into town just as they had done all week. It wasn't like riding with a young man in his courting buggy. They were on their way to help people affected by a disaster. They were not on a date. Yet a happy sense of anticipation gripped her.

Joshua had chosen to harness Tilly that morning. The mare stepped along brightly in the ground-eating trot that Standardbreds were famous for. Traffic along the rural highway was heavy for a Saturday morning. It seemed that people from all over were converging on the town in cars, pickups and wagons. Mary saw several license plates from neighboring states.

A large flatbed truck with a bulldozer on the

bed followed them at a crawl for a half mile before it could pass on the hilly road. Joshua pulled over to give the traffic more room as it flowed by them. The large white van that passed them last was from Pennsylvania. It was loaded with young Amish men and women.

"It hasn't taken long for the word to get out among the Amish." He guided Tilly back to the center of their lane when the way was clear.

"The town will be grateful for the extra help. I heard yesterday that the Mennonite disaster relief people were on their way."

"They always find a way to help. I'm sure more Amish will be coming, too. The recovery will take months."

"So many groups rushing to help. It restores my faith in people."

He cast a sidelong glance her way. "Do you doubt there are good people?"

"Sometimes. I know it's wrong, but it's hard to accept people at face value."

"Our faith teaches us otherwise, but I know what you mean. It's hard for me, too."

"You are thinking about your brother and the people he became involved with."

"In part, but I was thinking about something else."

She waited for him to elaborate. He didn't. "Something that happened to you?"

He shook his head. "It's not important."

"Now you have made me doubly curious."

He glanced at her and smiled. "I see where Hannah gets it."

"Which is a polite way of telling me to mind my own business. Very well. Tell me about Bowmans Crossing. What's it like?"

"It's nowhere near as big as Hope Springs. It's more a collection of farms and small Amish-run businesses than a true town. When my family first settled in the area, they built a house by the river and ran a ferry crossing for their neighbors. That's how the place got its name. There is a bridge over the river now, but folks still call it Bowmans Crossing."

"You said your parents farm there."

"*Ja.* My *daed* was the youngest son, so he inherited the home farm. Two of his brothers own a buggy-making business. Another sells harnesses."

"Do they live nearby?"

"All within a mile. You can't throw a rock in any direction without hitting one of my cousins."

"It must be nice to have a big family."

"I guess it is. I've never known anything else."

"What will your father do with the land your mother inherited?"

"I'm not sure. My youngest brother will

inherit the home place, so maybe one of us will take over my great-uncle's property here."

Would Joshua be sent to farm it? The idea that he might settle in the area brought on mixed emotions—happiness that he might remain close by, worry about what that would mean if her attraction to him grew unchecked.

"Delbert mentioned that you moved to Hope Springs a few years ago. Where was home before that?"

"I grew up near New Philadelphia." The edge of Hope Springs came into view and she quickly changed the subject. "I hope the television cameras are gone."

"I only see one."

A gray-haired man in the uniform of a county deputy stopped them. He held a large clipboard. "Are you residents?"

"We are volunteers," Joshua said.

"Names?"

He wrote down their information and then pulled two yellow bracelets from a box. He handed them to Joshua. "I know the Amish don't wear jewelry of any kind. You don't have to have this on, but you need to have it somewhere on your person so you can prove you are here legitimately. The numbers match your name, so be sure and check out with a sentry when you leave town. Please accept my gratitude for coming to help. I went to school here, way back when. It breaks my heart to see so much of the town in ruin."

"The town will recover." Mary tried to comfort him with her words.

"I know it will. There are some mighty fine, mighty strong people here. If we didn't know that before, we sure know it now." He waved them through.

She looked at Joshua. "I'm to meet Betsy and some of the other women at the Red Cross tent in the park. You can drop me at the inn. What will you be doing?"

"The volunteers were asked to meet in the park, too. Most of the streets have been cleared and all of the damaged roofs have been covered, so I think we're starting a house-by-house cleanup of debris."

"When our shift is over, Betsy and I will lend a hand."

He glanced at her feet. "Did you wear sturdy boots? You'll need gloves, too."

"I'm wearing Ada's work boots and two pairs of socks so I won't get blisters. I have gloves in my pockets. I'll be fine."

"Where is the buggy maker's shop? I promised Hannah I would see about getting her wagon fixed and she reminded me this morning that I hadn't done it."

"Follow the street that runs behind the Wadler Inn to the west side of town. You can't miss Levi Beachy's place. I should warn you about the twins."

Joshua laughed. "I've already been warned about Atlee and Moses. I'll try not to fall prey to one of their pranks. The way folks talk, you would think the tornado was their doing." He pulled Tilly to a stop in front of the inn.

Mary got down before he could help her. "It wouldn't surprise me if they had something to do with it. Can you deliver these supplies to the Red Cross tent, too?"

"I sure can. See you later." He slapped the reins on Tilly's rump and drove away.

Betsy came out of the inn with a huge load of towels in her arms. "The two of you looked quite cozy riding together."

Mary knew she was being teased. "It's not a very big cart. I would look cozy if I'd only had a broom with me."

"Not that cozy. Is he still staying with you and your grandmother? What does she think about him? He's single, after all."

"Ada has her eye on Delbert Miller for me."

Betsy's eyebrows shot up. "You can't be serious."

"She's getting desperate. I'll be twenty next Sunday, so the pressure is on."

"I know that feeling." Betsy adjusted the load in her arms.

"How is Alvin's mother?" Mary took half the towels from Betsy and they began walking toward the park. The persistent sounds of chain saws had been replaced by the rumble of heavy machinery and countless hammers boarding up windows and repairing roofs. The smell of diesel exhaust hung heavy in the air.

"She's getting as antsy as Ada. Lots of talk about the grandbabies everyone else is having while she may be in the grave before she has any. She told Alvin the tree branch that slid off the roof and hit her was God's way of telling him to speed things up."

"And is he?"

Betsy paused and looked around to make sure they couldn't be overheard. "He proposed last night."

Mary's mouth fell open. "He did? What did you say?"

"I told him I'd rather that he ask me because he loves me and not because his mother got hit by a tree limb. It wasn't that big a branch."

"You said no?"

"Not exactly."

"You said yes? You were going to stay single until you were twenty-five. I've heard you say that a dozen times."

"I know what I said. I told him maybe. It would be nice to have a home of my own. When I see my sisters Clara and Lizzie with their babies, I think it would be nice to have a baby, too."

"Take my advice. Don't make the same mistake I did. Have a husband first. It makes life a lot less complicated."

"Don't tell me you see Hannah as a mistake, because I won't believe you. No one could love their little girl more than you do."

"I never think of her as anything but the most precious gift God could give me. I made my share of mistakes, but she is my redemption. How did Alvin take your answer?"

Betsy sighed heavily and shook her head, making the ribbons of her *kapp* dance. "Not well. He has stopped speaking to me."

"He'll get over it. He's head over heels for you."

"I thought he was, but now, I'm not so sure."

They reached the tent. It was busy as volunteers manned stations of water, ice and food. The hum of a generator could be heard outside. Orange electric cords stretched across the floor, held down with strips of duct tape. A small television at a desk in the back flashed with images of the destruction taken by helicopters and reporters on the ground.

There was little time to talk as Betsy and Mary passed out food, water and hot beverages to a steady stream of volunteers. A few were merely sightseers, not interested in working. They had come to gawk. The rest, young Amish people from neighboring communities, college students and off-duty first responders from as far away as Kansas, were all there to give freely of their time simply because they wanted to help someone in need.

Moving tons of rubble was backbreaking work, as Mary learned after her four-hour shift at the tent ended. She was loading bricks from a collapsed chimney into a wheelbarrow when she saw Joshua approaching. She straightened and brushed her gloves together. "Did you get something to eat? They still have sandwiches at the food tent."

"I finished my break a few minutes ago. I'm on my way back to work, but I've been sent on a mission to find you."

"Me? What for?"

"I met a local fellow named Alvin. When he learned I was staying at your place, he enlisted my help to gather some information about a friend of yours."

"Betsy."

"*Ja.* He seems like a nice fellow, so I thought

I would help him out." Joshua began picking up bricks with her.

"Oh, dear. What exactly does he want to know?"

"Is she seeing someone else?"

Mary threw a brick in the wheelbarrow and glared at Joshua. "Of course she isn't. She's been seeing Alvin for ages."

Straightening with a brick in each hand, Joshua tipped his head to the side. "Then I am a little confused. I thought he wanted to go out with her."

"He wants to marry her."

"Then he should ask her."

"He did."

"Now I'm even more confused. Did she give him an answer?"

"She said maybe."

"Now I get it." He tossed his bricks on top of hers. "He's wondering if she is waiting for someone else to ask the same question. Otherwise, she would've said yes or no."

The wheelbarrow was full, so Mary grabbed the handles. "She said maybe because she isn't ready to marry. She wants her freedom for a while longer."

"Can I tell him that?"

"Since he hasn't figured that out for himself,

you can. And he should inform his mother." She began walking toward the street.

Joshua followed her with an armload of bricks. "I think I'll draw the line at telling him what he should say to his mother. I don't mind helping a fellow find out if a girl is interested, but this relationship sounds more complicated than I am equipped to handle."

She grinned at him. "It's a wise man who knows when he is in over his head."

Joshua stopped in his tracks. She had such a pretty smile. It made her eyes sparkle, and his heart stumbled over itself when she aimed it at him. He knew for a fact that he was getting in over his head because he sure wanted to see her smiling a lot more. At him.

He hurried to catch up with her. "What are we doing with these bricks?"

"We're stacking them on a pallet in the driveway. They'll be taken to be cleaned and reused to repair Mrs. Davis's chimney by a local bricklayer who has volunteered his services."

"Nice guy." Joshua began stacking the bricks tightly together.

"I think so, too. Mrs. Davis doesn't have family to help her. She is watching us from the window, by the way. I have heard she's afraid to leave her home and hasn't been out since the storm."

"It had to be frightening to see this destruction up close and then have the place overrun with strangers."

Joshua glanced toward the house. The curtain at the window fell back into place. A second later, it parted again as a yellow cat settled itself on the window ledge to watch them. Joshua casually bent to tie his bootlaces and glanced covertly toward the window. A small white-haired woman holding a gray cat in her arms pulled the curtain aside again.

A tall *Englisch* man came striding down the street toward them. "Let me give you a hand with those."

Mary straightened, put her hands on her hips and stretched backward. "This is the last of the unbroken ones. Joshua, this is Pete Metcalf. He's the bricklayer I was telling you about."

"Good to meet you." Pete held out his hand. Joshua shook it.

Mary pulled off her gloves. "How are your wife and family getting along?"

"It's still crowded at the inn, but we're really grateful that we have a place to stay. Thank you for insisting we go there. The baby is doing great. She is the center of attention when she's awake. It's like having two dozen babysitters. The only problem is that we can't find our cat. The kids have been all over town and they are brokenhearted. We even took your suggestion and checked at the veterinary clinic, but she wasn't there."

"You should have the children check with Mrs. Davis. She is a cat lover. I think she has taken in some strays. I noticed some open cans of cat food on her steps."

Pete hiked a thumb toward the house. "Mrs. Gina Davis, the lady whose chimney I'm fixing?"

"Ja."

"I'll go ask her now."

"Nee," Mary said quickly, stopping him. "Send the children."

"Why the kids?"

"They are less frightening than a strange man would be. When people are scared and anxious, small children can help them overcome that fear."

He shrugged. "Okay, I'll have them come over."

When he left, Joshua moved a step closer to Mary. "Why didn't you ask her if she had their cat?"

"I don't need a place to stay or someone to care for me or about me. Mrs. Davis and Pete's family both need those things. Maybe a cat can bring them together."

He tipped his head slightly and regarded her

with a bemused expression. "You know she has their cat, don't you?"

"The children came by the Red Cross tent earlier. They were showing people a drawing of a gray cat with three white feet. The little boy drew it since they didn't have any photographs. They were hoping someone had seen her."

"And we just saw Mrs. Davis holding a cat like that."

Mary grinned. "It might not be the same cat. Then again, it might be. Or it might be another cat that needs children to love."

"And my family thinks I'm the optimistic dreamer. They should meet you. They would adore you."

Mary blushed a rosy red.

The moment the words were out of his mouth, Joshua regretted them. What was he doing? He wouldn't be in town for more than a few more days. He had no business implying he wanted her to meet his family. That wasn't going to happen. He was on parole. Her father was an *Englisch* lawman. His family wouldn't be comfortable with that.

The last thing he needed was to fall for this woman with a sweet daughter and an even sweeter smile. It couldn't work between them. As much as he liked her, he wasn't able to trust her father.

Maybe when his sentence was up. Maybe when he wasn't afraid of being sent back to prison. Maybe. All his life he'd been taught to avoid the *Englisch* and shun their worldly ways except when he had to do business with them. His time in prison had taught him to fear them. Mary's father was polite and it was clear he loved Mary and Hannah, but Joshua couldn't bring himself to trust the man. He avoided Nick when he could and stayed silent when he couldn't.

Stepping away from Mary, Joshua said, "I should get back to Alvin. I'm sure he's on pins and needles waiting to hear what I learned."

"Tell him Betsy needs time to think over his offer. I'm sure she loves him, but I think she's afraid to admit that. She isn't ready to settle down now, but she will be one day."

"I'll tell him that. *Danki*. How will I find you when I'm done for the day?"

"I'll be in the Red Cross tent with Miriam or Nick."

Joshua nodded. Hopefully, her father would be out working elsewhere.

Just then, Pete returned with his son and daughter. He waited at the foot of the steps while they went up to the door and knocked. When the door opened a crack, the little boy held up a piece of paper. "This is our cat, Socks, and she's missing. Have you seen her? We miss her an awful lot."

The door opened a little wider. Joshua strained to hear the woman's reply. "I have seen a cat like that, but she's not so fat."

The boy turned his picture around to stare at it. "I'm not a very good artist. Where did you see her?"

"Wait here." Mrs. Davis closed the door. When she opened it again, she held the gray cat in her arms.

The little girl began jumping and shouting, "That's Socks. Socks, we found you." She held up her arms.

Mrs. Davis came out on to the porch and sat on a green painted bench. "She's been very scared. You have to be quiet so that you don't frighten her even more."

The little girl cupped the cat's face between her hands and rubbed their noses together. "I missed you so much."

The little boy stroked the cat who was purring loudly. "Thank you for taking care of her."

The little girl gathered the cat in her arms. "I'm going to take you home now."

"Except we don't have a home," her brother reminded her gently.

From the bottom of the steps, Pete spoke. "We appreciate you taking care of Socks. Our house was destroyed and we are staying at the inn. Could you continue to look after her until we find someplace more settled? We can pay you to board her, although it will be a few days before I have the money from our insurance settlement."

"But, Daddy, Socks wants to stay with me." His daughter looked ready to cry.

"I know, honey, but we don't have a safe place to keep her. A lot of people are coming and going at the inn. She could get out and get lost again. You don't want that."

"No."

Mrs. Davis rose to her feet. "She can stay here. Why don't you children come inside and visit with Socks for a while? I have other cats. Would you like to meet them? If that's okay with your father," she added quickly.

"That would be great. Thank you. I'll get this mess in your yard cleaned up as soon as possible. Do you have other damage?"

"My attic window is broken."

"There's a fellow with glass and cutting tools over by the school. I'll let him know you need some work done."

Mrs. Davis opened the door and followed the children inside. Joshua gave Mary a wry smile. "You were right. Children can help."

"The way having Hannah with us helped you when we were in the cellar."

That surprised him. Had Mary noticed how fearful he'd been that day? "It did help. I hate small places, but knowing Hannah and you needed me to remain calm gave me a way to control my fear."

Mary fisted her hands on her hips. "I reckon I'll help Pete clean this yard so the children can play out here without getting hurt."

"I'm on my way to the Hope Springs Fellowship Church."

She smiled at him. "We'll meet up again later."

Joshua thought a lot about Mary as he walked toward the church. She had a knack for understanding people who were afraid. She saw ways to help them. His admiration for her grew. When he reached his destination, he saw a dozen men working on the roof of the white clapboard church that had sustained serious damage. The young pastor was the only *Englisch* fellow among the Amish men with their shirtsleeves rolled up. Joshua stepped into line and carried a bundle of shingles up a ladder to where Alvin was hammering them into place. He stopped working when he saw Joshua.

"Well? Is she seeing someone else? Did you find out anything?"

"Mary was very helpful. Betsy is not seeing anyone other than you. She isn't in a hurry to marry, and pressing her probably isn't the right thing to do." Joshua laid the bundle of shingles where others could reach them.

"I don't understand why she won't marry me. Her sisters are all married. That can't be the reason. Even her grandfather recently married, so it's not because she has to take care of him. I don't get it."

"Mary says to give her time." Joshua pulled his hammer from the tool belt Alvin had loaned him and began setting the shingles in place. The two young men, both the same age, were quickly becoming friends after meeting that morning at the command center, where they'd been assigned to the same tasks for the day. The rat-a-tat-tat of hammers filled the air around Joshua as he and the other men made short work of the project.

Alvin drove the next nail in with unnecessary force. "I'm tired of waiting. There are a lot of young women who would be pleased to go out with me."

"And yet none of them are Betsy."

Alvin put his hammer down. "That's the truth. I like you, Joshua Bowman. You've got a good head on your shoulders."

"There are others who don't think so."

"How long are you staying?" Alvin positioned the next shingle.

"I need to be back in Bowmans Crossing

before Thursday. I'll have to hire a driver or take the bus if one goes that way."

"With all the people that have showed up to help, I'm sure someone from your neck of the woods is here. There's a message board at the inn. You can put a note there asking for a ride."

"Good idea. *Danki.*"

"Don't mention it. It's the least I can do after sending you to question Mary. I appreciate it. I could've asked one of my friends or cousins, but I thought since you knew Mary so well she might tell you something she wouldn't tell them."

"I don't know her that well. We only met the day of the tornado."

"Is that so? But you're staying with her and her family."

Joshua related the story of their night in the cellar while they worked.

Alvin slipped the last shingle in place. "She's a nice girl. She befriended Betsy when she and her sisters moved here. Have you got a girl back home?"

"I don't. You're blessed to have found the right one."

Alvin shook his head. "Only if she'll marry me."

"Don't give up. Looks like we are done here. What do we do now?"

"Go back to the command center and see what else they need us to do."

Would Mary be there by now? Joshua discovered he was eager to find out. It was sad—no matter how hard he worked at convincing himself he should stay away, he was ready to jump at the chance to see her again.

He followed the group of men back to the center of town to find where to go for their next project. He spied Mary standing by Miriam and Nick at the back of the Red Cross tent. Both women wore shocked expressions. Nick's angry scowl made Joshua hesitate, but Mary's distress pulled him to her side. "What is it? What's wrong?"

She looked at him with tear-filled eyes. "I was on the news. My face was on television and so was Hannah's."

Chapter Nine

Mary noticed Joshua's perplexed expression. He didn't understand how serious this was. How could he? She hadn't told him anything about her former life. She was starting to like him too much. She didn't want him to know what a foolish girl she'd been.

What if Kevin Dunbar had seen her picture? Numbing fear made her heart pound. If he had, then he knew where she lived. Where Hannah lived.

"I'm going to have them stop airing it." Nick pulled his cell phone from his pocket and stormed out of the tent. As upset as she was, Mary couldn't help noticing Joshua's relief at Nick's departure. Did he dislike her father? Was it because he was the English law? Many Amish distrusted Nick in the beginning, but they soon came to see he was honest and sensitive to their ways even when those ways conflicted with the law he was sworn to uphold.

Miriam's phone went off. She read the text and shoved the phone in her pocket. She gripped Mary's hand. "I'm needed at the medical tent. I'll be back as soon as I can."

After Miriam left, Joshua took a step closer. His eyes were filled with compassion. "Your church members will understand that you weren't seeking notoriety. The news cameras must have captured many Amish people." He pointed to the television. "Look, there's Delbert helping clean out someone's house."

The camera was panning a particularly hard-hit area of homes. It wasn't a close-up of Delbert, but his size made him recognizable. There were several Amish men and women in the scene. Joshua believed she was upset because the Amish shunned being photographed. She wanted to explain but she couldn't. Miriam and Nick had decided years ago to keep her past and her old identity a secret. The fewer people who knew, the safer she and Hannah would be.

Besides, Mary didn't want to involve Joshua. This was her father's business. She needed to let him handle it.

"It isn't just you, Mary. I see the girls from the singing, too. Their faces are recognizable. You are worried for nothing."

She drew a deep breath. "You're right. It's foolish to be upset."

After all, what were the chances that Kevin had been watching? He was still in prison.

A few moments later, Miriam came back. "Nick said he has taken care of it. The clip won't run again. Joshua, would you take Mary home? I'm sure that Hannah is missing her, and I'd like someone to check on Ada. I have to stay. I'm the only nurse on duty right now."

"I don't mind at all," he said quickly. He seemed relieved to have something to do. "I'll go get the cart and meet you out front in a few minutes."

Mary clutched Miriam's arm when Joshua was out of sight. "Do you think Kevin might have seen this? Would he have television in his cell?"

"Not in his cell, but there is a common room where the men can watch programing the warden deems suitable. This news channel is probably one of those. Even if he saw this, he's still behind bars. He can't hurt you."

"I'm afraid and I shouldn't be. My life is in God's hands. It has always been. I know that. He is my protection. He is Hannah's protection."

Miriam pulled Mary close for a quick hug. "I believe that, too, but I can't help worrying about you. Kevin may have friends on the outside.

There is a multitude of strangers here. I think it would be best if you didn't come back to help."

Mary pulled away, shamed by her doubts. "These are our friends, Miriam. I can't hide when I see how much still needs to be done for our community. To remain at home would be cowardly."

"My Amish upbringing tells me you are right, but I've been married to a cop for too long. I know that evil exists."

"But it is not stronger than our faith."

"You are so brave."

Mary smiled at her adoptive mother. "I've had good examples to follow."

Miriam's phone went off again. She quickly scanned the text. "I have to go. More people have been hurt by nails and saws, falls and falling limbs in the last two days than were injured by the tornado itself. Let Ada know that Nick and I won't be by tonight or tomorrow morning. Nick is worn to the bone. He needs what little rest he can get. He's been going nonstop since this whole thing happened. If I can steal an extra half hour of sleep for him, I'm going to do it. He gets cranky when he's sleep deprived."

"I'll tell her."

"*Danki.* Give Hannah our love."

"I will." Miriam left and Mary went outside to wait for Joshua.

Betsy stood by a card table handing out donated gloves. She was pointedly ignoring Alvin standing nearby. Mary walked over to her and whispered an old Amish proverb. "Keep your words soft and sweet in case you have to eat them."

Shooting Alvin a sharp look, Betsy turned to Mary. "That's why I'm not talking to him. At all. Where are you going?"

"Home. Miriam thinks Ada needs a break from watching Hannah, but I'll be back Monday morning. What about you?"

"I'll be here. My sister Lizzie has decided the family needs something fun to do after all this work. She proposed we have a picnic by the lake next Saturday. I'd love it if you would join us."

"That's very kind. I know Ada is always happy to visit with your grandmother."

"*Goot.* I'll see you tomorrow at the prayer meeting. It's at Adrian Lapp's place. At least they didn't have any storm damage."

"Am I invited to the picnic?" Alvin asked. He had moved closer while they were talking.

"I reckon," Betsy replied without enthusiasm.

He stuck out his chin. "If I'm not busy, I might come."

"Don't fret about it. If you can't make it, you won't be missed." Betsy threw down the pair of gloves she held and marched away.

Joshua pulled up with the cart. Mary gave Alvin a sympathetic look. "Don't worry, Alvin. She'll come around."

He glared at Betsy's retreating back. "The question is will I be around to see it." He walked away in the opposite direction.

Mary climbed in beside Joshua and he set Tilly in motion. "Things are still not going well for them?"

"*Nee*, and I'm afraid Betsy is just digging in her heels now."

"That's a pity. Are you okay?"

She knew he was referring to the newscast. "I am. It's not likely that there will be trouble because of it. It was just a shock. I had already been scolded for being too forward and then to see my face plastered on the television screen was upsetting." It was true, but it wasn't the whole truth.

"I don't find you forward. Who scolded you?"

Mary folded her hands in her lap and kept her eyes down. "Miriam. She is right—sometimes I am too bold in my speech. She thinks that Nick is a bad influence on me, but he isn't."

"I don't find you bold at all. I find you refreshing."

She didn't know what to say to that. She noticed a cardboard carton beneath his feet and decided to change the subject. "What's in the box?"

"Hannah's wagon."

"I'm surprised that Levi Beachy had time to fix it."

"He didn't, but he let me use his tools."

"Did you?" How kind was that? In the midst of all this destruction, he'd made time to repair her daughter's toy. He was a good, kind man.

"It didn't take long. I had such a big breakfast that I didn't need a lunch break."

"I remember you just picking at your breakfast this morning. I thought maybe you didn't like my cooking."

That was the wrong thing to say. Now he would think she was fishing for compliments.

"Your cooking is good, but it's not like my *Mamm's*."

That put her firmly in her place. "I'll try to do better."

He grinned. "You don't have far to go."

Okay, that was nice. "Thanks again for fixing Hannah's wagon. She loves pulling that thing around."

"I noticed she had some paper chickens she wanted to take to market. Does she have other animals?"

"She used to have a cow, but its head was accidently removed by Bella."

He laughed. "Better a paper cow than the real one."

Mary smiled at him, her fright forgotten for a moment as she relaxed in his company. "You haven't tried to milk Rosie. You might change your opinion about that."

He laughed again and her spirits rose. Joshua Bowman was good company inside and outside of a cellar.

Seeing the worry fall away from Mary's face made Joshua happy. He still didn't understand why she had been so upset about appearing on the news. There had to be more to it than what she was sharing with him. He'd seen the flash of fear in Nick's eyes, too, before anger replaced it.

Joshua was curious, but it wasn't any of his business, so he kept quiet.

A car honked behind them. Joshua urged Tilly to a speedier pace. The road was still filled with traffic and many drivers grew impatient when they had to creep along behind an Amish wagon or buggy. He didn't want to cause a wreck. Unfortunately, it meant they arrived at Ada's farm that much quicker and his time alone with Mary was cut short.

And soon the rest of his time with her would be cut short, too. He would have to head home by Wednesday at the very latest. It wouldn't do to miss his first meeting with his parole officer, even for another day in Mary's company.

When they reached the farm, he stopped the cart by the front gate and got out. He held out his hand to help her down. Her fingers closed over his with trusting firmness. Hannah darted out of the house, letting the screen door slam behind her. Tilly flinched at the sound, jerking the cart. Mary lost her balance. She would have fallen if he hadn't caught her by the waist and pulled her against him. She clutched his shoulders to steady herself.

He gazed into her wide eyes as he slowly lowered her to the ground, reluctant to let her go. His hands spanned her tiny waist with ease. Color bloomed in her cheeks. An overpowering urge to kiss her hit him. What would she do if he tried?

Hannah shot down the porch steps. "Joshua, you're back. Did Levi get my wagon fixed?"

Joshua slowly released Mary. Her hands slid down his arms in a soft caress before she stepped away. He drew an unsteady breath and turned his attention to Hannah. Ada was at the screen door watching them with a knowing little smile on her face.

Feeling foolish, he gave Hannah his full attention and dropped to one knee to address her. "I went to the buggy shop, but as I suspected, Levi was too busy to work on your wagon."

Her hopeful expression fell and her lower lip slipped out in a pout. "Oh. Well, that's okay. Lots of people need their real buggies fixed. I can pretend my shoe box is my wagon for a little while longer."

"I'm glad to hear you say that, Hannah. It means you believe in putting the needs of others before yourself."

She tipped her head slightly. "It does?"

"It does. Thinking of others has its own rewards." He rose to his feet and withdrew the box from beneath the seat. Setting it on the ground in front of her, he waited for her to open it. Mary looked on with a pleased expression.

Hannah glanced up at him. "What's this?"

"A reward for putting others first."

She opened the flaps of the cardboard box. "My wagon! It did get fixed."

She pulled it out and then stared in the box with a puzzled frown. "Someone left their toys in here."

He grinned. "They are your toys. I made them for you."

"You did?" She reached in and came out with a handful of wooden animals.

"Look, *Mamm*, Joshua made me a cow and two horses and three pigs, and here is Bella!"

The toys were little more than crude wooden cutouts, but he'd had a chance to sand them smooth. They were recognizable animals even if they weren't detailed. "Do you like them?"

"They are *wunderbar*! Did you make some chickens?"

"I didn't because you already had some." And because they might have taken more skill than he could muster with Levis' jigsaw.

She loaded the animals in her wagon and ran toward Ada. "*Mammi*, look what Joshua made for me."

"They are very nice. Did you thank him?"

"*Danki*, Joshua."

"You're welcome."

Ada held open the screen door so Hannah could come inside. "Joshua is making both my girls smile today."

Feeling pleased with himself, he propped his arms on the gate. "Ada, you are the only Kaufman woman I want smiling at me."

"You are a flirt." She rolled her eyes and blushed before she disappeared into the house.

"Only because you tempted me with your fried chicken," he called after her.

He turned to put the horse away and found Mary watching him with her arms crossed and a tiny smile curving her lips. "How do you do that?"

"How do I do what?" He strolled back to stand

in front of her with his thumbs hooked under his suspenders.

"How do you make us all like you so easily?"

Joshua leaned closer to gaze into her sky-blue eyes. He saw the chasm opening under his feet, but he was powerless to keep from falling in. Why did the first woman to turn him inside out have to be a sheriff's daughter? "Do you like me?"

"I can't decide."

"Guess that means I'll have to try harder." He leaned closer still, but instead of trying for the kiss he wanted, he slipped past her, grasped Tilly's bridle and led the mare to the barn. He knew Mary was watching.

Inside the barn, he found Oscar waiting for him in the first box stall. The big brown horse whinnied a greeting. He limped forward and Joshua saw the large dressing covering his hip. "Looks like the vet took care of you."

He led Tilly into an adjacent stall, unharnessed her and began to rub her down.

The barn door opened and Ada came in with a basket full of bandages and ointments. "Before you flustered me, I was going to tell you that your horse arrived."

"I'm sorry I teased you, but your fried chicken is the best. I mean that. Better than my mother's, and that takes some doing."

"Stop with the flattery."

"If I must."

"The vet sent instructions on how to take care of your horse's injury and some supplies. I'll leave them here." She put them on a workbench beside the barn door.

"Danki."

Her face grew serious as she walked toward him. "I know it is not our way to interfere in the lives of our young people, but I'm an old woman with a bad heart, so I hope you will forgive me."

"For what?"

"Are you a free young man?"

He stopped brushing the mare and stared at Ada. His stomach flip-flopped. Had she found out about his prison record? "What do you mean?"

"Don't flirt with Mary unless you are prepared for her to take you seriously."

Laying his currycomb aside, he came to the stall gate and leaned on it with his arms crossed. "I would never knowingly hurt Mary."

"I'm sure that's true, but she has endured many heartaches. I don't want to see her suffer another if I can help it. Do you know what I mean?"

"I like Mary. I think we can be good friends."

"But not more than friends?"

"I have to return home. It may be a long time before I can come back."

She sighed deeply. "I'm glad you are honest about it. You are a likable young fellow, but don't encourage her if you don't mean it with all your heart. I have never seen her smile at anyone the way she smiles at you. I don't want to see her get her heart broken. Supper will be ready soon."

"Can I ask you something, Ada?"

"Ja."

"Is Mary still mourning Hannah's father?"

"She does not mourn him. He did not treat her well, but through him, God gave her Hannah, and for that gift we are all grateful."

"Why hasn't she gone out with some of the local fellows?"

"Because a man must win Mary's trust before he can win her heart, and she does not trust easily."

Ada left the barn and he mulled over her words as he finished taking care of Tilly. Was he being unfair to Mary? He liked her. He wanted to spend more time with her. If she felt the same, what harm was there in their friendship?

He wasn't prepared to admit his feelings were stronger.

He left the stall and picked up the supplies for Oscar. He briefly read through the vet's instructions. It was simple enough. He entered Oscar's stall with the intention of changing the dressing as per the vet's instructions. He noticed the grain in the horse's feed bucket hadn't been touched, but his nose was wet from getting a drink.

"What you doing?"

Joshua looked over Oscar's back to see Hannah had climbed to the top of the stall gate and was watching him. "I'm checking to make sure Oscar is comfortable. He's in a strange new place and he's had a lot of scary things happen to him."

"He looks okay to me."

"Looks can sometimes be deceiving. He hasn't eaten anything, but he has been drinking water, so that's good. I think he'll be okay in a day or two."

"*Mammi* says you are going to be leaving soon."

"That's right. I have to go home."

"You are coming back, aren't you?"

"I hope I can. Will you look after Oscar for me until he can come home?"

"I think *Mamm* should do that. He's pretty big."

"What is it that you think I should do?" Mary asked as she leaned on the gate beside her daughter. Joshua's heart jumped up a notch, as it always did when he caught sight of her. He was kidding himself. What he felt was much more than friendship.

"Joshua wants you to look after Oscar until he comes back because he's going to be leaving soon."

Mary met his gaze. "I reckon I can do that, if he will show me what needs to be done."

"I was about to change the dressing, if you want to watch. The vet left me detailed instructions."

She opened the gate and slipped into the stall, making Hannah giggle as she swung it wide and then closed it. Hannah grinned at her. "That's fun. Can we do it again?"

"After Joshua shows me what needs to be done." Mary moved to stand near him. She kept her arms folded tightly across her middle. He tried to keep Ada's warning at the forefront of his mind. He didn't want to hurt Mary. He would be more circumspect in his dealings with her.

"First thing is to remove the old bandage."

She stepped up beside Joshua to read the paper he held. Her nearness caused him to lose his train of thought. "Then what?" she asked.

He forced his attention back to the horse. "The vet stitched the wound, so you want to check and make sure none of the stitches look infected." He pulled the dressing off and revealed a swath of shaved skin with a neat set of sutures down the center. The cut itself was about eight inches long.

"It looks good to me."

"Me, too." He softly pressed along the wound. "You want to check for hot spots or lumps that would indicate an infection is forming deep in the tissue." Yellowish fluid oozed from the lowest stitch when he pressed beside it.

Mary placed her hand next to his and followed with an examination of her own. "I don't feel anything unusual. What about this drainage?"

"The vet says we need to wash it down with cool water and he suggests putting some petroleum jelly on the skin below where it is seeping. He sent along some ointment to put on the dressing to keep the edges of the wound moist. Mostly, I'm worried about Oscar rubbing it against the boards when it starts itching."

Mary rubbed her left wrist. "I remember how much they itched before the doctor took them out."

"You've had stitches? I never have. What happened?"

She looked away and tugged her cuff lower. "I got cut with a piece of glass."

"On your wrist? That could've been serious."

"I was fortunate." She folded her arms again and wouldn't make eye contact.

Something told him there was more to the

story, but he didn't press her. "Other than a dressing change every other day, he shouldn't need anything special. The vet doesn't want him out where he can run, but I hate to see him confined to a stall."

"I can walk him."

"That would be great." He applied the ointment and a clean dressing, and then patted Oscar's shoulder.

"Do you know when you'll be leaving?" Mary followed him out of the stall.

He swung the gate wide several times, making Hannah laugh as she held on. He plucked her off and set her on the floor. "I must be home by Thursday. I'll stay as long as I can."

Hannah skipped out of the barn ahead of them. Mary walked slowly. "When do you think you'll be back?"

He had to be honest. He stopped walking and she paused beside him. "I'm not sure when I'll be back, or if I'll be back."

"I see." Some of the light in her eyes died.

"A lot depends on the man I'm meeting on Thursday. If I can't return, my father will send one of my brothers to collect Oscar."

"I hope you come back." She bit her lower lip and looked down, as if she were afraid she had said too much.

He lifted her chin with his fingers until she

was looking at him. "I hope I can, too. But I can't make you any promises."

She laid her hand against his cheek. "I'm not asking for a promise."

The longing in her eyes was too much for him to resist. He leaned forward and gently kissed her.

Chapter Ten

Mary knew she should turn aside, but she didn't. Joshua gave her a chance to do just that. He hesitated, only a breath away from her. She didn't move. She wanted to know what his mouth would feel like pressed against hers. She closed her eyes.

His lips were firm but gentle as he brushed the corner of her mouth. She tipped her head slightly and he took advantage of her willingness. His kiss deepened and it was more wonderful than she had imagined, than anything she remembered. Her heart raced. She gripped his shoulders to steady herself and kissed him back.

A few seconds later, he pulled away. She opened her eyes to stare up at him. His face mirrored her wonderment. She didn't know how to react or what to say.

Regret filled his dark eyes. "I'm sorry, Mary. I shouldn't have done that."

She pressed her hand to her lips. They still tingled from his touch. "Don't be sorry."

She turned and raced out of the barn, determined to regain her self-control. Something she couldn't do when he was near.

After all this time. After all the heartaches she had endured, the Lord had finally sent someone to make her believe in love again.

Only she knew it couldn't be love she felt. It had to be infatuation. She barely knew Joshua and he barely knew her, but for the first time in years, she believed it was possible to care about a man and have him care about her in return. A man who was kind and generous. Someone who could make her heart flutter with just a look.

When she reached the house, she paused and looked back. He was standing in the barn door watching her. He didn't look happy. Her common sense returned, pulling her silly girlish fantasy out of the clouds.

He was sorry he had kissed her. He was leaving. By his own admission, he might not come back. She was a fool to let her feelings get so far out of hand. Miriam had warned her to think with her head and not to let her emotions rule her. She hadn't listened.

It wouldn't happen again.

* * *

It couldn't happen again.

If Joshua had known how much a simple kiss would change his relationship with Mary, he would never have given in to the impulse.

Supper was strained. Mary wouldn't look at him. She barely spoke. She barely touched her food. Even Hannah seemed to notice that something was wrong. She kept glancing from her mother to him with a questioning look in her eyes, but she didn't say anything.

Ada kept up her usual running chatter. Had Mary told her what he'd done? He didn't think so. If Ada thought he was trifling with Mary, he was pretty sure that she would sic Bella on him. He half believed that he deserved it. After professing that he would never hurt Mary, he'd gone right ahead and made a very stupid move.

The thing was, he didn't regret that kiss at all.

Mary's smile was sweet, but the taste of her lips was even sweeter. They were soft and delicate, like the petals of a rose.

And he had to stop thinking about it right this second. It couldn't happen again.

When he went into the living room to read the Bible after supper, Mary excused herself, claiming a headache, and went to bed early.

Hannah played quietly with her wagon and wooden animals for an hour, and then Ada took her up to bed. Joshua was left alone with his thoughts. They weren't happy ones. His impulsive gesture might have cost him a friendship he valued deeply. Was there a way to make it up to her? Would apologizing again help? Or only make things worse? He was afraid to find out.

He wandered into the kitchen. He missed having tea with Mary. He missed the quiet, intimate moments they shared across the red-and-white-checkered tablecloth. Leaving the kitchen, he climbed the stairs. He glanced at Mary's closed door, then kept walking until he reached his room. He didn't write home. Instead, he lay down on the bed and folded his arms behind his head as he tried to figure out his next move. The full moon rose and cast a bright rectangle of light through the window. He watched the moonbeams' slow crawl across the floor for hours and still didn't have an answer.

Sunday morning dawned bright and clear and Mary was thankful she could finally get out of bed. Attempting to sleep had been a futile exercise until the wee hours.

She saw Joshua's door was open when she stepped out into the hallway. His bed was neatly made and empty. He was already up, too. She paused at the top of the stairs. What would she say to him? What would he say to her?

Could they pretend the kiss had never happened and go back to being friends?

She was willing to try.

She had breakfast well underway by the time he came in from taking care of the animals. She smiled cheerfully. "Good morning. How is Oscar?"

A bemused expression flashed across his face before he turned to hang his hat on a peg by the door. "His hip is draining more. I changed the dressing again."

"Do you think we should have the vet out to look at him?"

Joshua washed up at the sink. "I don't think it's that bad. If it's not better by Monday, then maybe we should."

After drying his hands on a towel, he folded it neatly on the counter. "Is your headache better?"

"All gone."

"Mary, about yesterday. I'd like to explain."

Pasting a false smile on her face, she said, "It was just a kiss, Joshua. It wasn't my first one. In case you haven't noticed, I have a daughter."

"I just want you to know that I didn't mean to offend you. I value your friendship. I hope I haven't lost that."

"You haven't lost a thing. I'm still your friend." She turned away. It was too hard to keep up the pretense while he was watching.

"I'm thankful for that. It won't happen again."

Oh, but she wished it would. "Go ahead and pour your own coffee. I'm going to get Hannah and Ada up. We'll have to hurry if we don't want to be late for church." There was plenty of time, but she left the room, anyway.

Since they hadn't yet been able to purchase a new buggy, they journeyed in the cart to the home of Adrian and Faith Lapp about three miles away. The main doors of the red barn had been opened wide. Men were unloading backless wooden benches from a boxlike gray wagon the congregation used to transport them from home to home on the day of the services. A number of men recognized Joshua and called out a greeting. Atlee and Moses Beachy had been put in charge of the horses. They came up to the cart as Joshua helped Mary down.

Ada gave the young men a stern look. "No tricks from you boys today."

Atlee and Moses smiled at each other. Atlee said, "Everybody has been telling us that. A good joke is only funny when you least expect it. We couldn't get away with anything today. Everyone is watching."

Ada poked her finger toward them. "I'm keeping my eye on you just the same. Any funny business and you'll have to answer to me."

Mary tried to hide her smile, but she caught

Joshua's eye and saw he was struggling to keep a straight face, too. A giggle escaped her. Ada could no more keep up with those two boys than she could fly, but that didn't stop her from giving them what for.

Joshua managed to cover his chuckle with a cough. He handed Mary the baskets of food from the back of the cart. "Find me when you're ready to leave. It doesn't matter to me how long we stay."

The service would last for at least three hours. Afterward, a light noon meal would be served. Afternoons were usually spent visiting with friends and neighbors while the children played hide-and-seek and the teenagers got up a game of volleyball. Families didn't normally leave until late afternoon. If the hosting family was having a singing that night, many of the young set would remain until dark.

Ethan Gingerich came up to Joshua. "How is your horse faring?"

"The wound is still draining more than I would like. Have you any suggestions?"

The two men walked away discussing equine medicine. Mary sighed deeply. Joshua seemed right at home among them. It was a pity he was leaving. She would miss him dreadfully.

Ada grasped Mary's arm to steady herself as

they walked across the uneven ground. "What's the matter, child?"

"I just realized that Joshua is going to find out today that I've never been married."

"Why do you say that?"

"Because I will be sitting in my usual place with the unmarried women. He'll know I wasn't married to Hannah's father."

"And how will he know the women around you are single? He doesn't know them."

"He knows Betsy. We always sit together."

"Well, isn't it better that he finds out sooner rather than later?"

"I know, but I don't want him to think badly of me."

"Our mistakes cannot be undone, child. We face them, we admit them and then we strive to do better. The sins of your past were all forgiven when you were baptized. If Joshua thinks less of you, then he is not a man to worry over, he's a man to be forgotten. There are plenty of Amish men in this community who would prize you as a wife."

"I'm not sure that's true, but you are kind to say so. Only I don't fancy any of them."

Ada turned to face her. "And do you fancy Joshua Bowman?"

"I'm not sure, but I think I do."

Mary thought Ada would begin shouting for

joy. She was always pressing Mary to find a man. To her surprise, Ada ignored her comment and said, "Let's take this food into the house and enjoy praising our Lord on this beautiful day. We have much to be thankful for. I wonder who will preach the service since Bishop Zook is still in the hospital?"

After delivering the food to the kitchen and chatting briefly with the women gathered there, Mary, Hannah and Ada went out to the barn and took their places on the benches provided.

The sun shone brightly beyond the barn doors. They had been propped open to catch the warm rays on the cool spring morning. Rows of wooden benches in the large hayloft were filled with worshipers, men on one side, women on the other, all waiting for the church service to begin. Large tarps had been hung from the rafters to cover the hay bales stacked along the sides. The floor had been swept clean of every stray piece of straw.

Mary sat quietly among her friends with Hannah beside her. Glancing across the aisle to where the men sat, she caught Joshua's eye. He was near the back among the single men. He smiled at her and she smiled back shyly. If he realized the significance of where she was sitting, it didn't appear to bother him. Had she been worried about nothing? When would she learn to leave her fears in God's hands?

As everyone waited for the *Volsinger* to begin leading the first hymn, Mary closed her eyes. She heard the quiet rustle of fabric on wooden benches, the songs of the birds in the trees outside and the occasional sounds of the cattle and horses in their stalls below. The familiar scent of alfalfa hay mingled with the smells of the animals and barn dust as a gentle breeze swirled around her. She opened her eyes and saw a piercing blue sky above the green fields outside. It was good to worship the Lord this close to His creations.

The song leader started the first hymn with a deep clear voice. No musical instruments were allowed by their Amish faith. Such things were seen as worldly. More than fifty voices took up the solemn, slow-paced cadence. The ministers, the deacon and the visiting bishop were in the farmhouse across the way, agreeing on the order of the service and the preaching that would be done.

Outsiders found it strange that Amish ministers and bishops received no formal training. Instead, they were chosen by lot, accepting that God wanted them to lead the people according to His wishes. They all preached from the heart, without a written sermon. They depended on the

Lord to inspire them. Some were good preachers, some more ordinary and some, like Bishop Zook, were truly gifted at bringing God's word alive on Sunday morning.

The first song came to an end. The congregation sat in deep silence. The Lord's Day was a joyful but serious day. Everyone understood this. Many in the community had suffered, but God had spared many more. All of them were here to give thanks.

After a few minutes of silence, the *Volsinger* began the second song. When it ended, the ministers and the visiting bishop entered the barn. As they made their way to the minister's bench, they shook hands with the men they passed.

For the next several hours Mary listen to the sermons delivered first by each of the ministers and then by the bishop. They spoke of sharing the burdens that had been placed on the community. She tried to absorb the meaning of their words. There had been many times when she felt burdened by the vows she had taken, but today wasn't one of them. She belonged to a special, caring people.

She closed her eyes and breathed deeply. This day she felt the warmth of God's presence. She gave thanks for the goodness He had bestowed upon her and her family and begged His forgiveness for all her doubts and faults.

Facing the congregation, the bishop said, "Galatians, chapter six, verses nine and ten. 'And let us not be weary in well doing: for in due season we shall reap, if we faint not. As we have therefore opportunity, let us do good unto all men, especially unto them who are of the household of faith.'

"The Lord has made it clear that it is the duty of everyone present to aid our members in need. As you know, Bishop Zook was injured in the storm. He remains in the hospital, but by God's grace he will soon be released. We will be taking up a collection for the medical bills he can't meet. His barn was also destroyed in the same storm. I have met with other area bishops and we are planning a barn raising for him a week from Monday. Everyone is invited to help to the extent that they are able." He gave a final blessing and the service was over.

The scrabble of the young boys in the back to get out as quickly as possible made a few of the elders scowl in their direction, including Ada. Mary grinned. She remembered how hard it was to sit still at that age. It was harder still because the young people knew they would be spending the rest of the day visiting with their friends and playing games. Although the young girls left with more decorum, they were every bit as anxious to be out taking advantage of the beautiful spring day. She let Hannah follow them.

Mary happened to glance in Joshua's direction and caught him staring at her. All the other men were gone.

Betsy elbowed her in the side. "Will you stop looking at that man like you are a starving mouse and he is a piece of cheese?"

Mary rose to her feet. "I'm not a starving mouse."

"You could've fooled me." The two of them went out together and soon joined the rest of the women who were setting up the food. The elders were served first. The younger members had to wait their turn. When Joshua came inside to eat, Alvin was with him. Betsy saw him, muttered an excuse and quickly left the room.

Alvin put his plate down. "I reckon I've lost my appetite."

He left and Joshua looked at Mary. "Is there anything you can think of that would aid his cause? He's miserable. He's been talking about her nonstop for the last half hour."

"Betsy is miserable, too. I don't know how to help."

"I might have an idea. It's my turn to have a plan, right?"

She smiled. "I think it's my turn, but you go ahead."

"Is Betsy the jealous type?"

"I wouldn't know. Alvin has been stuck to her side ever since they met. She's never had to worry about him straying."

"Let's see how she reacts if he shows an interest in someone else."

Mary bit her lower lip. "I don't know. That doesn't seem right."

"If this blows up in our faces, it's your turn for a plan."

"Oh, make it worse and then hand it to me. *Danki*. What girl will go along with this? Don't look at me."

"Just make sure Betsy is where she can see the barn door on the south side in half an hour. Can I borrow your traveling bonnet?"

"What for?"

He gave her a big grin. "Because my helpers didn't bring theirs."

"I have no idea what you are talking about, but I left mine on the seat of the cart."

"Okay. Thirty minutes."

"South barn door."

"Right." He winked and went out.

Betsy returned shortly. When it was their turn to eat, they carried their plates outside and joined Betsy's sisters on several quilts spread in the shade of an apple tree. The alpacas that Adrian and Faith raised were lined up at the fence watching the activity. Mary found them adorable, especially the babies. The adults, with their freshly shorn bodies and fluffy heads, were comical. The south barn door was in easy view from where she was sitting.

"Betsy, where is Alvin?" her sister Lizzie asked.

"I don't know, and I don't care," Betsy declared.

Her three sisters shared shocked looks. Clara, the oldest, gaped at Betsy. "Since when?"

"Since ages ago. I don't have to share everything with you just because you're my sisters."

Greta touched Mary's arm. "Did you know about this?"

"I know she's been miserable since he stopped talking to her."

"I have not. And he didn't stop talking to me. I stopped talking to him."

Mary saw Joshua and Alvin standing just inside the barn door. The bottom half of the split door was closed, but the top was open. A tall woman in a black bonnet was standing with them. She was turned so Mary couldn't see her face. She appeared to be in an animated conversation with Alvin.

Lizzie noticed at the same time. "He's not having any trouble talking to that woman. Who is that?"

Betsy swung her head around to look. "I don't know."

Alvin laughed at something the woman whispered in his ear. Her bonnet dipped and her shoulders jiggled as if she were giggling. Clara said, "She's very tall. I don't know who it could be."

Joshua stepped out of the barn and came toward them. Alvin slipped his arm around the woman's shoulder and they disappeared from view inside the barn.

Betsy shot to her feet. "Who was that with Alvin?"

Joshua shrugged. "I didn't catch the name, but they seem to know each other well."

He sat down beside Mary. "Are you about ready to go?"

She tried to keep a straight face. "Not yet."

Betsy fisted her hands on her hips. "Is it one of those Pennsylvania Amish girls that came to help in town? She should stay in her own state."

Joshua shook his head. "That's unkind, Betsy. Alvin was just being nice."

"I saw how nice he was being. I'm going to give him a piece of my mind."

"But you aren't speaking to him," Mary reminded her.

"You're right. I'm not." Betsy sat down, but

she couldn't keep her eyes off the barn. Alvin and his friend never reappeared.

Later, when they were getting ready to leave, Joshua was helping Ada into the cart when Atlee and Moses brought Tilly to them and hitched her up. Ada scooted to the far edge of the seat. "You boys were good today. I'm glad to see you've grown out of your need to play pranks."

Moses grinned at her. "I wouldn't say we've outgrown it."

Atlee handed Mary a bundle of cloth. "Thanks for the use of your bonnet. Alvin found it very becoming on my brother."

The boys punched each other in the shoulder and walked off laughing. Ada shook her head. "I'm glad they aren't mine."

Mary smoothed out her bonnet and took Hannah as Joshua handed her up. "Really? Moses, Alvin and my bonnet? That was your plan?"

He climbed in and took the reins. "I think it worked. Betsy was stunned. At least Alvin knows she isn't indifferent."

"You got her attention, I'll give you that."

"Now all Alvin has to do is keep it." He slapped the reins against Tilly's rump and the mare took off.

Relieved that his relationship with Mary seemed to be on the mend, Joshua was eager to return to work in Hope Springs. On Monday, he and Mary made the trip again. There were fewer volunteers in town. The initial storm and media coverage had brought in hundreds of people wanting to help. Now that the nitty-gritty of rebuilding was getting underway, there was less need for general cleanup and more need for skilled carpenters. The Amish and Mennonite workers remained as the backbone of the recovery effort.

After leaving Mary at the Wadler Inn, Joshua crossed the now barren blocks toward the church. He and several others would be rebuilding the portico that morning. As he passed by Gina Davis's home, he saw she was out pruning her rosebushes. Pete's children were playing in the yard. The front door of the house opened and a woman with a baby in her arms called for the others to come in. He saw Pete on the roof setting the last of the chimney bricks into place. Pete saw him and waved. "How's it going?"

Joshua stopped and tipped back his hat. "Not bad. And you?"

"I'm done here. I'll start at the school tomorrow. I've been hired by the school district to repair the building. It was an offer I couldn't refuse."

"The laborer is worthy of his hire. Are you still staying at the inn?"

Pete gathered his tools and came down the ladder. "Actually, we're staying with Mrs. Davis until we can get a new house built. It's working out for both of us."

Exactly as Mary had hoped it would. Joshua touched the brim of his hat. "Have a *goot* day."

He started to walk away, but Pete stopped him. "You might want to keep an eye out for anything odd. They told us in the town meeting this morning that some of the stores have been looted. The police have set up a tip line folks can call if they see something. Just when it seems the goodness of mankind toward one another is overwhelming, a few have to prove there are still miserable people out there."

Shaking his head in disbelief, Joshua walked on. Instead of following the winding street, he took a shortcut through a wooded area that surrounded the rocky outcropping behind the church. A small stream cut through the woods. It led to the bubbling spring that had given the town its name. There was a small bridge over the brook behind the church, but he had no trouble jumping across using a couple of convenient stones. He was about a block from the church when he saw two men slipping through the trees ahead of him. Something in their stealthy demeanor caught his attention. He watched as they entered the back door of a vacant house with faded paint and boarded-over windows that had fallen into disrepair years before the tornado arrived. He was tempted to walk on, but his curiosity drew him to follow them.

He approached the house and had his hand on the back doorknob when he heard voices coming from a broken basement window off to the side below him. "I stashed the weed here. Nobody's gonna check an old wreck like this place. How much do you want?"

"How much do you have?"

"Enough. If you want stronger drugs, I can get that too. I borrowed some from the pharmacy last night. The place was easy pickings. Their security system didn't even have power."

Joshua's skin crawled when he realized what was going on. He took a step back and his heel crunched a piece of broken glass.

"What was that? Check it out." The voice became a harsh whisper.

Joshua walked away quickly and hurried out to the street. At the corner, he saw Nick in his patrol car. Joshua hesitated. Should he tell Nick what was going on? Would Nick assume he was involved?

It would be better to say nothing. It wasn't Amish business. It had nothing to do with him. He hurried on toward the church. A few minutes later, he heard the sound of a siren behind him, but he didn't look back. He kept his head down and walked faster. He only slowed when Nick shot past him without stopping. Joshua blew out a long breath and waited for his racing heart to return to a normal pace.

It took him and his coworkers three hours to finish the new entryway for the church. Pastor Finzer came out of the rectory to view the finished project. There were tears in his eyes.

"Gentlemen, I can't thank you enough for your work here. It's wonderful to see the house of the Lord ready to welcome worshipers again. A little paint and elbow grease by yours truly and I don't think people will know the difference between the old and the new parts of the structure. It's beautiful."

He shook everyone's hand. "Please let me buy you lunch at the Shoofly Pie Café. It's the best Amish cooking for miles around."

Knowing that Mary was working at the inn that day, Joshua agreed and walked along with a group as they headed that way. Passing the section of woods where he had seen the men, Joshua slowed to see if Nick had gone that way. There was no sign of him.

The pastor noticed Joshua's interest. "That place belonged to the family that founded this town. It's a shame it was allowed to fall into ruin."

"I saw two men go in there earlier."

"Teenagers, perhaps. They've been known to hold parties there. I'll check it out."

The thought of the gangly young pastor stumbling into a dangerous situation forced Joshua to reconsider keeping silent. He stopped walking. "They weren't teenagers. I got the impression they didn't want to be seen."

Pastor Finzer stopped, too. Concern creased his brow. "Are you sure?"

"I heard there has been some looting around town."

"Sadly, that's true. Perhaps I should mention this to the authorities."

"You must do what you think is best. The fellow staying with Gina Davis said there is a tip line folks can call."

"That's right. I almost forgot. Go on to the café. I'll catch up with you." The minister walked rapidly back toward the church and Joshua breathed a sigh of relief.

At the inn, he checked at the front desk and learned Mary was running an errand. She wasn't expected back for half an hour. He found a seat at the café counter, ordered lunch and waited for Pastor Finzer to join him.

A hand clamped down on his shoulder. "Step outside right now," Nick growled.

Chapter Eleven

Joshua wanted to knock Nick's arm aside, but resisting would gain him nothing. He should have told Mary about his record when he had the chance. It would've been better coming from him than from her father. Now it was too late.

"I said, come outside."

Joshua turned on the bar stool. "Say what you need to say here. I am not ashamed."

"Outside!" Nick walked out of the building. Joshua followed slowly. He didn't have a choice. At least he wasn't being hauled away in handcuffs.

The sheriff didn't stop walking until he was half a block up the street. Then he turned on Joshua. "I knew there was something about you the minute I laid eyes on you. If I hadn't been so busy with this mess, I would have run a background check on you sooner. Not many Amish men turn up in my database. Imagine my surprise when Joshua Bowman was at the top of the list when I checked this morning."

Joshua pressed his lips shut. Nick didn't want to hear anything he had to say.

Nick glared, but drew a deep breath. "Have you told her?"

"I thought I would leave that to you."

"Don't get smart with me. Have you told Mary that you're a convict?"

"That I was wrongly imprisoned? *Nee.*"

"I didn't think so."

"I was going to tell her. Not that I expect you to believe me."

"You were picked up for dealing drugs. What do you know about a burglary last night at the pharmacy?"

Joshua folded his arms and glared. "If I know something, I must be involved. If I'm involved, that means I violated my parole, and I'm on my way back to prison, which is exactly what you want, isn't it?"

"Where did you get that chip on your shoulder?"

"Your justice system gave it to me."

Nick reined in his temper with visible difficulty. "I skimmed through your case file."

"Then you know everything. I won't waste my breath explaining."

Folding his arms over his chest, Nick relaxed slightly. "It left me with some unanswered questions. I would've handled the investigation differently."

"My story would've been the same no matter who asked. I didn't do the things they accused me of doing."

"Just like that, I'm supposed to believe you? You had a dozen chances to tell me you are out on parole. Why didn't you?"

"Because I knew exactly how you would react. Like this. Besides, I didn't see what difference it made. I came to look over some property for my father. I didn't choose to be trapped with Mary, but I started liking her. And this community. After I saw the extent of the damage here, I wanted to help these people rebuild."

"I think you're done helping. Hope Springs can get along fine without you."

"Don't you mean Mary will get along fine without me?"

"You're a smart fellow. That's exactly what I mean. Mary has had enough trouble in her life. She doesn't need to get involved with you."

"I happen to care for Mary a lot. If she were your *Englisch* daughter, I would say that you are right. But Mary is Amish. She knows that forgiveness comes first. She knows a thing that is forgiven must also be forgotten."

"You don't know anything about Mary."

Joshua reined in his own rising temper. "I know her better than you think. I also know you want to protect her."

"That's right. That's why you are leaving. I have a car waiting that will take you to Ada's place so you can pick up your stuff, and then my deputy will take you home. I'm also going to let your parole officer know that you were here without his knowledge. He's not going to like that, and he's going to keep a closer eye on you from now on."

Joshua strove to put his bitterness aside. He didn't want this animosity between himself and Mary's father. Not if there might be a future with her. He hung his head, trying to be humbled before God and this man. "When my sentence is finished, may I come back?"

"I'd rather you didn't."

Joshua looked up. "Because you don't want the criminal element in your town? Or because you don't want Mary seeing some guy you don't like? It's her choice. The Amish understand that. They don't interfere in the courtship of their children."

"Someday when you have a daughter, remember this conversation." He pointed up the block where an unmarked white car was waiting. "There's your ride. Get going."

* * *

Mary learned that Joshua had been looking for her when she returned from her errand. She checked in the café, but he wasn't there. She combed the area she thought he might be working in several times without seeing him. When she spotted Delbert cutting lumber at the back of the grocery store across the street, she approached him and waited until he finished the cut and the saw fell silent. "Delbert, have you seen Joshua? He was looking for me a while ago and now I can't find him."

"I saw him talking to the sheriff. They went that way." He pointed up the block.

"Danki."

She walked in that direction and saw Nick at the drugstore on the next corner. He was standing with his deputy, who was busy writing a report. The store owner was gesturing wildly. There was no sign of Joshua. She walked up to Nick. "I'm sorry to bother you, but have you seen Joshua?"

"He's gone home," Nick said without looking at her.

"Back to the farm?"

"Back to Bowmans Crossing."

"I thought he wasn't leaving until Wednesday."

"Something came up and he caught an early lift."

"What came up?" She tried to wrap her mind around the fact that he was gone.

Nick looked at her then. "You knew he was going to leave sooner or later."

Sooner or later, yes, but not without saying goodbye. Mary turned away to hide her distress. What a foolish woman she was to think she meant something special to him. "You're right. I knew he was leaving. I just didn't want him to go."

Tears stung her eyes as she walked away from Nick. When she turned the corner and there was no one to see, she broke down and sobbed.

Joshua received a heartfelt hug from his mother when he arrived home. No one had expected him until Thursday. His father and brothers were all out working in the fields. He looked forward to doing the same. To getting back to a simple life with plenty of hard work and little time to mourn the loss of Mary's company.

His mother gestured toward the table. "Sit down. I've just made some brownies. We have been reading about the damage at Hope Springs in the newspapers. It must be terrible."

"It is. The community is making progress, but a third of the homes were destroyed. Electricity has been restored to many of the English businesses and homes that are left, but some of them are still living Amish."

That made her chuckle. "It's good to have you home. Will the town recover?"

"The people are determined. There's still a lot of cleanup that needs to be done. Mary thinks it will take years for the place to look normal again. I think she's right."

"Mary is the woman you wrote about? The one you were trapped in the cellar with?"

"She's the one." He tried to remember exactly what he'd said about her. Probably too much. She occupied a central place in his mind.

His mother got down a plate and began cutting her brownies. "Is she pretty, this girl you couldn't leave behind?"

"Not as pretty as you, and I did leave her behind." He bitterly regretted that he hadn't been allowed to tell Mary goodbye. Would she think he didn't care enough to find her, or would Nick tell her the truth? Was she grieving or was she relieved to have Joshua Bowman out of her house and her life? Would he ever know?

His mother put a plate in front of him. "What will you do now?"

"I want to go back to Hope Springs. There is still so much work that needs doing." And Mary was there. Mary and Hannah, the two people who had come to mean the world to him.

His mother took a seat across from him. "Your father and I have been talking about that."

"You have?"

"Our bishop made a plea for supplies and money to aid the Amish folks there. You know they will share the financial burdens among themselves, but the expenses will be high and some families will suffer because of it. We must help if we can. Your brothers have agreed. I wish I could go along, but your father and your brothers could not do without me. I would like to meet your Mary."

"She's not my Mary and there is something I haven't told you about her."

"So serious. What is it?"

"She is adopted. Her parents are *Englisch*."

"That is not a terrible thing, although it is unusual."

"The woman that adopted her is married to Sheriff Nick Bradley."

Sitting back, his mother stared at him with wide eyes. "Perhaps we should not mention this to your father just yet."

"As much as I want to go back, it isn't up to me. I'll need to convince Officer Merlin it isn't a risk to let me go there. I don't think he'll agree. Nick Bradley doesn't want me seeing Mary."

"Is she a good Amish woman?"

"She reminds me a lot of you."

"I could be a better Christian."

"Mary isn't perfect, but she has an Amish heart. She is a good mother. She cares for her elderly grandmother with tenderness. She is sometimes outspoken, but she repents when she steps over the line. She would do anything for her friends and neighbors in need. *Ja*, she is a good Amish woman."

Better than he deserved. Maybe he shouldn't go back. Maybe this was God's way of telling him that she was better off without him.

"Let us pray about this and wait to see what the Lord wills. Your father can be a very convincing man. I should know. He convinced me to marry him when I had three other perfectly good offers."

Joshua laughed. "*Mamm*, were you a wild girl with a string of fellows?"

"I was. Until I wed. Eat your brownie and don't fret. God has a plan for us all. We must have faith in that."

"Why wasn't I informed that you were away from home?"

Officer Oliver Merlin sat at the kitchen table in the Bowman home on Thursday morning as promised. He finished the last bite of a cinnamon roll and licked his lips. Joshua's father and mother sat with him. Joshua was too nervous to sit in one place. He leaned against the spotless kitchen cabinets. He knew his brothers would be hovering nearby outside.

"My son was only doing what dozens of other young Amish people were doing. He was helping those in need. It was God's will that he was in Hope Springs when this disaster struck. He was not involved in any crime."

Officer Merlin dabbed his face with a napkin, then folded his hands together and leaned on his forearms. "I am not your son's enemy, Mr. Bowman. Nor am I your enemy. I am required to keep detailed records of my parolees' activities. My job is to see that Joshua can become a functioning member of society and stay out of trouble."

"Would you like another cinnamon roll, Oliver?" Joshua's mother pushed the plate in his direction.

"Don't mind if I do. These are just about the best I've ever had."

"*Danki.* You are too kind."

Isaac frowned at his wife before he leaned forward, too. "You can put my son back in prison with a word."

"My opinion can sway the court for him or against him, that's true, but it's his behavior that forms my opinion and that is what a judge will evaluate."

"My son is already a good member of our Amish community. He adheres to our ways. He needs no judge but God."

"I appreciate your religious convictions. I admire the Amish. I don't want to be intrusive, but I don't have the all-seeing eye of God. I need to observe Joshua at home as well as at work. I may show up at any time. I can even visit his friends to make sure they aren't involved in criminal activities. Joshua is motivated to do well, but he has a chip on his shoulder where law enforcement is concerned."

"Can you blame me?"

Joshua moved to brace his arms on the edge of the table and glare at his parole officer. "I didn't do anything wrong. I was there to convince my brother to come home. The police who arrested me wouldn't listen. No one believed me. The prosecutor made it sound as if I had been making drugs for months. The woman who said I did this, under oath, did it to get her own sentence reduced. People acted like we were freaks. I saw the papers—Amish Brothers Arrested for Cooking Meth by School. Buggies Used to Smuggle Drugs to Rural Teenagers. I wasn't with my brother until two days before I was arrested. Do I have a distrust of English law enforcement? *Ja*, I do."

It wasn't until his father laid a hand on his

shoulder that Joshua realized he was shaking with anger. His father spoke quietly in Pennsylvania Dutch. "We forgive them. We forgive them all as our Lord forgave those who persecuted Him unto death."

Joshua nodded, shamed by his outburst. "Forgive me."

"I'm not here to retry your case, Joshua. Do innocent men go to jail? Yes, they do. Do guilty men go free? All the time. I'm here because I don't want you to go back to prison. I want your family and your friends to understand that. They may think they are protecting you by clamming up when I ask questions, but they aren't. If we can't be honest and forthcoming with each other, this may not work. I don't want that. I like it when my people stay out of trouble."

Joshua's mother placed her folded hands on the table. "What about Luke? Can he come home soon?"

"I can't make that determination. I can report that he has a stable home environment waiting and his family will be supportive if I'm called on to testify."

Joshua walked to the window. He stared outside without seeing his father's farm. It was Mary's face he envisioned. "Will I be allowed to return to Hope Springs and continue with the recovery efforts?"

"Do you have an address where you will be staying?"

"I'm not sure. There's a place called the Wadler Inn. They are giving rooms to workers. I'm sure you can find their telephone number. They will know how to reach me if I find lodging elsewhere."

"I'd like a little more concrete information."

Joshua turned away from the window. "The town was nearly leveled. Some people still don't have electricity. They don't have water. Many don't even have a roof over their heads. I'm sure I'll be staying with an Amish family, but the Amish don't have telephones. The phone number for the inn is the best I can do. If you say I can't go, then that is that. But know there are people in desperate need there."

He wouldn't be able to stay with Ada and Mary. He was sure Nick wouldn't allow it. Joshua turned back to the window. How could he miss them all so deeply after only a few days? He missed Hannah's energy and Ada's cooking and teasing. He missed everything about Mary, but mostly he missed her smile.

Officer Merlin folded his black notebook and zipped it closed. "All right. You can return to Hope Springs. Check in with Sheriff Bradley when you get there. If I decide to drop in and see how you're doing, I'll expect the people at the inn to tell me where you're staying."

"Sheriff Bradley doesn't want me in his town. I was…I was seeing his daughter."

Oliver rose to his feet. "I noticed he was quite sharp on the phone."

"He can be more so in person."

"It's a free country. You have limits because of your parole status, but Sheriff Bradley can't stop you from returning to Hope Springs if I give my approval. However, I would suggest you give serious thought to avoiding his daughter. I'll be at the inn in Hope Springs on Saturday evening. You will be there."

"I will." Joshua hoped his face didn't reveal his relief. He would see Mary again. He would explain everything and pray that she understood and forgave him. He would find out if the Lord had a plan for the two of them. He prayed it was true. All he wanted was to see her again.

When Officer Merlin drove away, Isaac sighed heavily. "I wished only the best for my children. How have I failed them?"

Joshua came and laid a hand on his father's shoulder. "You did not fail us. We have failed you."

"Life is long. I pray I will see all my sons around this table again one day." He rose to his feet. "I made arrangements with the *Englisch* horse hauler to get your animal brought home, but he can't pick him up until Saturday. Would you write to Ada Kaufman and tell her that?"

"I will." Could he explain what happened in a letter to Mary? No, it was better to see her face-to-face.

After his parents went into the living room. Joshua stayed in the kitchen. Samuel came in carrying the mail. "Was the *Englischer* satisfied with your behavior?"

"Well enough, I reckon. He'll be here again in two weeks and he will check on me in Hope Springs."

"*Daed* and I have loaded a wagon with furniture and lumber for you to take with you. It's not a lot, but we have some to spare for those less fortunate." His voice trailed away as he stared at the envelope in his hand.

"What is it?" Joshua asked.

"It's a letter from Luke. He's never written before."

"That will please Mother."

Samuel held it out. "It's not addressed to Mother. It's addressed to you."

"To me? Why would he write to me and not to *Mamm* or *Daed*?"

"You'll have to open it and see." Samuel laid the letter on the counter. "I've got a rocking chair to finish and a harness to repair. I could use your help."

"I'll be out in a minute." Joshua picked up the letter and tore it open. It was short and to the point—Luke needed to see him. There was no other explanation. Something was wrong.

"You'll get over him. Men can't be trusted. Women are better off without them."

"You don't mean that, Betsy." Mary looked up from the supplies she was restocking in the Red Cross center and glanced around. The temporary tent had been taken down and the relief center now occupied the basement of the town hall. A new truckload of donations had arrived that morning. The first boxes contained much-needed necessities like soap, toothpaste and shampoo. Some of the men, including Alvin, were setting up tables and folding chairs in the room down the hall that would serve as a place of relaxation and a meeting room when needed.

"Maybe I do mean it. Just a little. Some men can't be trusted. And those are the ones we are better off without."

Mary didn't feel better off without Joshua and she didn't want to talk about it. The ache was too new, too raw. She prayed that he would write and tell her why he left without a word. There had to be an explanation. "Does that mean you haven't made up with Alvin?"

Betsy glanced down the hall. It was empty. "He was flirting with another woman. You saw it."

"Betsy, you turned him away. He has been faithful to you for two years and you turned him away because you are afraid to commit to marriage. You tell him to go away, and when he does, that makes you angry? Do you know how ridiculous you sound?"

Betsy snapped the lid closed on a cooler filled with water bottles. "Okay. I didn't like seeing Alvin interested in someone else, but I don't know what I want. Do you?"

Oh, yes, she did. Mary wanted to see Joshua again. She wanted to know that the friendship and affection she thought they shared wasn't one-sided. She wanted to believe she could have a chance at a normal life and not have to live out her days alone. Joshua had opened her eyes to that possibility, but now he was gone.

"We aren't talking about me, Betsy. It doesn't make any difference what I want. Alvin is still here. You are the one who has a choice."

"But what if it's the wrong choice? How can I tell that I'll like him in ten years, let alone still love him in fifty years?"

"Ada says marriages are made in heaven, but husbands and wives are responsible for the up-keep."

"It's a wise Amish proverb, but what does it really mean?"

"It means you won't love him in fifty years if you aren't determined to love him every day from now until then. Answer me this. Can you see your life without him in it?"

"I don't know. I just don't know."

Alvin came around the corner with a set of folding chairs in his hands. He dropped them on the floor with a clatter. "I know what I want, Betsy Barkman. I want to have children with you and grow old with you and lie down in the earth beside you when my time comes. That's what I want. That won't change in ten years and it won't change in fifty years. Maybe you can see a life without me, but I can't see one without you. I love you, and I don't care who knows it!" He turned to look at the room but it was empty.

Mary hid a smile and picked up the supplies. "I'm going to take these to the closet."

Betsy snatched the box from her hands. "I'll take them. Alvin, would you give me a hand?"

His face turned beet-red and he rushed around the end of the counter to take the box from her. Together, they vanished into the supply room that was so full of donations there was barely enough room for one person, let alone two.

When they came out ten minutes later, Betsy's lips were puffy from being kissed and her cheeks were bright red. Alvin wore a look of bemused satisfaction. He picked up the chairs and hurried down the hall with them.

"Well?" Mary knew the answer. Betsy's eyes sparkled like stars in the night sky.

"A fall wedding. He loves me." She whirled around once and hugged Mary.

As happy as she was for her friend, Mary couldn't help the stab of jealousy that struck her. Would she ever find that kind of love?

Nick walked in through the front door, pulled off his sunglasses and came over to the two women. "How's it going?"

Betsy composed herself and gestured to the counter. "Two boxes of much-needed things like soap, and one box of shoes that contained two pairs of red high heels and six pairs of flip-flops. Not the best footwear for working in a disaster zone. What are people thinking?"

He chuckled. "We'll never know. Mary, I thought I would see if you'd like to join me for lunch. We haven't had a chance to spend much time together lately. I'm sure Miriam can join us."

Shaking her head, Mary said, "I'm not really hungry. You go on."

"Mary, you have to eat. He isn't worth getting this upset over."

She knew he meant Joshua. She looked down. "I'd rather not talk about it."

"He wasn't who you thought he was," Nick muttered.

She looked up quickly. "What do you mean by that? What aren't you telling me?"

Chapter Twelve

The following afternoon, Joshua once again faced the gray walls and high wire fences of Beaumont Correctional Facility. The driver his father had hired for the day agreed to be back to pick Joshua up in an hour. Although Joshua dreaded walking in the doors, it was considerably better to come as a visitor than it was to be a prisoner. He was searched and led into a small waiting room. A second door opened and Luke came in. His brother was all smiles, but Joshua knew something was up.

"It's good to see you, little brother. Mother's home cooking agrees with you."

"You're looking thin." Joshua sat down at the table.

"The food here stinks. You haven't forgotten that so quickly." Luke paced the room.

"What's up, Luke? Why am I here?"

"Maybe I wanted to apologize for getting you in trouble in the first place."

"I appreciate that. You know you have been forgiven. The family will welcome you—surely you know that."

Smirking, Luke said, "I know the Amish forgive sinners. I've heard it all my life."

"It's not something we say. It's something we do." Something Joshua was learning to do.

Luke looked at him sharply. "You're really beginning to sound like our old man."

"I pray that is true. Our father is devout and wise."

"Mom wrote that you've been working in Hope Springs."

"I've been helping with the tornado cleanup. There's still a lot to be done."

Luke brightened. "Are you going back?"

Joshua nodded. "Our family is donating some lumber and furniture and *Mamm* is sending canned goods. I'm headed back tomorrow with the wagon."

He hoped that Mary would forgive him for his sudden departure when he explained why he'd left without saying goodbye. She had the right to be upset that he hadn't told her about his prison time, but he believed she would understand. He was anxious to see her again. He dreamed of her at night and thought about her every hour of the day.

Luke sat down at the table. "That's just great. I was wondering if you met a woman there named Mary Shetler."

"*Nee*, the name isn't familiar."

Luke's left leg tapped up and down. There was a hollow look in his eyes. Joshua scowled at him. If he didn't know better, he would suspect Luke was using drugs again, but how could he get them in here?

Luke frowned and bit thumbnail. "That's too bad. I need you to do me a favor when you go back. I need you to find her."

"Why?"

"I've got a friend in here. His name is Kevin Dunbar. Joshua, he saved my life. There was a fight in the yard and I would have been stabbed if Kevin hadn't knocked the knife out of the guy's hand. I owe him. You understand that, don't you?"

"If he saved you, he was an instrument of God's mercy. I'm grateful for his intervention, but what does this have to do with finding someone in Hope Springs?"

"Kevin had a girlfriend, an ex-Amish girl. She was pregnant with his baby when he was locked up. She hasn't contacted him. His letters have all been returned unopened. He thinks she returned to the Amish. Her name is Shetler, Mary Shetler. He wasn't sure where she went. He had some friends looking for her in her hometown, but they never found her. He about gave up hope until he saw her on the news about Hope Springs."

"If she didn't answer his letters, maybe she doesn't want to see him."

"He still loves her. He respects her decision. He doesn't hold it against her. He just wants to know that they are both okay. Joshua, the man doesn't know if he has a son or a daughter. He's made mistakes, but he deserves to know his child is okay."

"She might not be living in Hope Springs. Many Amish came from other places to help. I don't know, Luke. The fellow is *Englisch*. His business is none of ours."

"You know it's important in here to have someone who can watch your back. This isn't Bowmans Crossing. Things can get ugly in here. This guy is my friend. He's helping me out."

"How?"

"He's taking care of me. Making sure I'm okay."

"Is he getting you drugs?"

"That's not a very Amish thing to say. He's going to get me a job with a couple of his old pals in Cleveland when I get out of here."

"Making meth again?"

"You are the suspicious one now. They run a salvage yard. I want to help a friend just the way you want to help the people in Hope Springs. Some of them are *Englisch*, too, aren't they? This is no different. All you have to do is ask around quietly and see if you can locate her. You don't even have to speak to her. He just wants to know that she's okay."

Joshua thought of Mary. He longed to know how she was. He hungered for any word of her. He could understand a man wanting to know his child and the woman he loved were safe and happy. "Okay, I'll ask around."

"Great. That's all you have to do. You are doing me a big favor. I owe you for this, little brother. When I get out of here, we are going to have some good times together, you and I."

"Does this mean you'll come home?" Joshua asked, fearing he already knew the answer.

Luke rubbed his face with his hands, shot to his feet and began pacing again. "You know the Amish life isn't for me. I don't want to be stuck in the Dark Ages. I want to be surrounded by life and fun."

"We Amish have life and fun all around us, Luke. We aren't stuck in the Dark Ages. We work hard and live a simple life so that we may be close to God and to each other."

"Like I said, you sound like *Daed*. So tell me about this girl you're seeing in Hope Springs. What's she like?"

"How do you know about her?"

"*Mamm* forwarded all of your letters. You know how she loves to keep circle letters going in her family. You sound quite taken with Mary Kaufman and her daughter, Hannah. Is Mary pretty?"

"She's very pretty and very sweet." His heart ached to see her again.

"And Amish. *Mamm* must be over the moon about it."

Joshua sobered. "Not as much as you might think."

"Why not?"

"It's complicated."

"What's complicated about love? It's spring. It's in the air, unless you're locked in this place."

"In my case, a lot. Mary is Amish, but she was adopted by an *Englisch* couple when she was a teenager."

"So?"

"Her father is the sheriff."

Luke burst out laughing and slapped the tabletop. "My ex-convict brother is dating the daughter of a sheriff. That has to be the funniest thing I've ever heard. What does her *daed* think about you?"

"Nick Bradley doesn't care for me."

"I can imagine. Are you going to call him Papa Nick after you marry his little girl, or will it always have to be Officer Nick? You might have been better off taking a ride in the tornado."

"I'm glad it's a joke to you. For me, it's serious."

"I'm sorry. I don't mean to tease you. All you have to do is ask around for Mary Shetler when you get back to Hope Springs and let me know as soon as you hear anything. Kevin is going to be paroled soon. You don't even have to come see me. Just call. Do this favor for me and I'll come home when I get out. I promise. What do you say?"

It was late in the afternoon by the time Nick turned into Ada's lane. Mary sat beside him quietly. Their relationship had become strained over the past few days and Joshua was the reason. Nick knew something about Joshua's sudden departure, but he wouldn't talk about it. Mary never doubted how much Nick loved her and Hannah, but somehow, his feelings about Joshua were driving a wedge between them. She hated it, but she didn't know what to do about it.

In the yard, she saw a wagon piled high with lumber. Two gray draft horses stood with their heads down at the corral fence. They looked as weary as she felt.

Nick stopped the car. "Looks like more Amish contributions are on their way to Hope Springs. It must be someone who knows Ada."

They opened the car doors and got out. Hannah came flying down the steps and threw herself into her mother's arms. "*Mamm*, guess what? Joshua is here. He came back."

Mary's heart stopped for an instant and then raced ahead as joy welled up inside her. He was back. He had come back.

It was hard to breathe.

She looked toward the porch and saw him standing with Ada. Mary choked back a sob. She was so happy she was ready to cry.

Joshua came down the steps with his hat in his hand. It was then she noticed that he didn't look happy to see her. He looked worried. Her joy ebbed away.

Nick moved to stand beside her and crossed his arms as he glared at Joshua. "I'm surprised to see you here."

"I just stopped to rest the horses and to let Ada know a horse hauler will be here Saturday to pick up Oscar. I'll be heading into town after I speak to Mary. If that's okay?"

The men were staring daggers at each other.

Mary's confusion grew. "Of course you can speak to me, Joshua. What's going on?"

His expression grew puzzled. "I wasn't sure you would want to see me after the things Nick told you about me."

"Things? What things? Nick, what's he talking about?" Something was going on, and she had no clue what it was. She didn't like the feeling. She put Hannah down. "Run inside and tell Ada to put on some tea, will you, dear?"

"Sure." Hannah dashed away.

Mary glanced at Joshua and saw confusion in his eyes. He was staring at Nick. "You didn't tell her."

"I thought I would leave that up to you if you had the courage to come back."

Mary fisted her hands on her hips. "Someone had better tell me what's going on?"

Nick looked down at the ground. "Don't make me regret this, Joshua. She is a pearl beyond price and more dear to me than my life. I don't know what I would do if anyone hurt her." He kissed Mary's cheek and walked to his vehicle.

He opened the door, but paused and looked back at Joshua. "I arrested a couple of guys on suspicion of burglary yesterday. We got a tip from Pastor Finzer about where they were staying. He said you had seen something suspicious. I appreciate it when citizens look out for each other. It makes my job easier." He got in and drove away.

Joshua looked ready to fall down. Mary rushed to his side. "Are you okay?"

"I believe I would like that tea now. I have a few things to tell you, Mary, and Ada should hear them too."

"Finally. Come inside." She took his arm and led him toward the house.

When they were settled in the kitchen, Mary sent Hannah to play in the other room. Ada glanced back and forth between Mary and Joshua without comment.

He drew a deep breath. "The reason I had to get home was so that I could meet with my parole officer."

Mary sucked in a sharp breath. Of all the things she expected him to say, this wasn't among them. Ada frowned. "What is a parole officer?"

Joshua gave her a lopsided smile. "He watches over people who have been released from prison early to make sure they are walking the straight and narrow."

Ada's mouth fell open. "You were in prison?"

Mary was equally stunned. "Why?"

"Do you remember me telling you about my brother? The one who left the Amish."

Mary nodded. "His name is Luke."

"Luke had been in and out of trouble for a while. His first arrest for drugs nearly broke my mother's heart. He went to jail and we thought when he got out that he would come home. But he didn't. My parents believed that he was lost to us. I couldn't accept that."

"Of course not. You love him," Mary said softly.

"I went to see him. I went to try and convince him to come home. He had gone from using drugs to making and selling them. I couldn't make him see how much he was hurting everyone. I couldn't get through to him. After two days, I gave up. Before I could leave, there was a drug raid. Luke had sold meth to an undercover cop. I was there when it happened. I wasn't making drugs. I wasn't using drugs. I wasn't selling drugs, but that didn't matter to the men who arrested us. The house was across the street from a school. I don't know how my brother could have been so stupid."

"Why would being near a school make a difference?" Ada asked.

"The penalty for endangering children is much higher."

Kevin had always made sure he stayed far away from them when he was selling drugs. Mary looked at Joshua. "Didn't your brother tell them you were innocent?"

"He did but no one believed him. No one believed me. The district attorney was eager to get a double conviction. One of the women Luke supplied was arrested on another charge. In exchange for a lower sentence, she testified that I had been helping Luke for months." He took a sip of his tea.

"She lied?" Ada stared at him in disbelief.

He set down his mug. "Drugs are a powerful and evil master."

Mary leaned toward him. "Why didn't you tell me this to begin with?"

"If you remember, you were trapped in a cellar with a total stranger and you were scared to death."

"And later? When we got out of the cellar?"

He stared into his tea as if it contained some important information. Suddenly, she knew the answer to her own question. "Nick."

Joshua nodded. "It seemed the wisest course was to keep silent. I wasn't sure if I had violated my parole by coming here. I *was* sure Nick wouldn't like the idea of a convict staying with you."

"He found out and that's why you left early."

"It was Nick's…suggestion."

Ada sighed and gave him a bright smile. "Well, you are back now and things are as they should be. I'll get fresh sheets for your bed."

Joshua shook his head. "There's no need. I won't be staying here. I'll come by to visit often, but I'm going to stay in town."

Mary reached across the table and laid a hand on his arm. "You can stay with us. I can handle Nick."

Joshua could barely believe the blessings the Lord had bestowed on him. Nick had not turned Mary against him. Joshua was guilty of misjudging the man. Mary and Ada accepted his explanation and were still willing to open their home to him. It was more than he had dared hope for. Until now, he'd cared for Mary and valued her friendship, but seeing the determination in her blue eyes sent a rush of deeper emotion through his chest. He was in love with her. It didn't matter that he hadn't known her long. He wanted to spend a lifetime getting to know her, earning her trust, providing for her and caring for her for the rest of his days.

That was his goal, but he knew he had to start with small steps. She liked him, but Ada had warned him that Mary grew to trust people slowly. "I'm sure you can handle Nick, but I don't want to cause friction between you. I would love to stay, but it's best if I go on into town. Besides, my parole officer will be checking in with me at the Wadler Inn."

He loved that she looked disappointed. "Okay, but you are staying for supper tonight."

"I can't, but I will be back tomorrow morning to do the chores and to finish fixing your corncribs, Ada. After that, I'll be working in town. But first, I have to deliver this lumber to your bishop's home before dark."

Mary pulled her hand away. "Your family's contribution is most generous."

He wanted to be alone with her. To show her how much he had missed her. He rose to his feet. "I should go check on my team. How is Oscar getting along?"

Mary shot to her feet with her hands clenched in her apron. "I was just going to change his dressing."

Ada smiled. "I thought you did that this morning?"

Mary blushed. "Did I? That's right, and I felt the drainage was worse, so I was going to check it again. Joshua, why don't you take a look and tell me what you think. It's your decision if we need to call the vet."

"Sure. I'll take a look at him." He followed Mary to the door.

Ada chuckled. "That's going to be the most pampered horse that has ever lived in my barn."

Joshua made a pretense of checking over his team before he entered the barn. As soon as

Mary came in behind him, he held out his hands. "I missed you so much."

She took his hands and squeezed them. "I missed you, too. I was so afraid I would never see you again."

He drew her into his embrace. She rested her cheek against his chest. For a long time, they simply held each other. He had never known such happiness. Unfortunately, he couldn't hold her forever. He lifted her chin and brushed a kiss lightly across her lips. "As much as I want to stay, I had better get on the road. I don't want to be driving my big wagon after dark."

"Promise me you won't vanish again without telling me where you're going."

"That's an easy promise to make."

"Thank you for your honesty in the house. I should be honest with you in return. There are things about me that you need to hear."

"They won't change how I feel about you."

"You won't know that until I'm finished."

Hannah came through the barn door. He and Mary quickly stepped apart. "*Mammi* wants to know how Oscar is."

He shared a knowing smile with Mary. "*Mammi* wants to make sure we are behaving ourselves." He tweaked Hannah's nose. "Oscar is fine. You have been taking good care of him. I missed you."

"I missed you, too. *Mammi* says we're going to have a picnic at the lake tomorrow for *Mamm's* birthday." She hopped up and down with excitement.

"That sounds *wunderbar*. I'm sure you'll have a good time."

"You can come with us." Hannah clapped her hands.

"Happy birthday, Mary. That's awful nice of you to invite me, Hannah, but I think the picnic is just for your family."

"Nonsense," Ada said as she came into the barn. "I expect you to join us. We aren't leaving without you. Not after all the work you have done in this community. There will be several families there, not just ours."

"Please say you'll come," Hannah begged.

"I don't see how I can refuse such a kind invitation." He caught Mary's eye. Maybe he could find some time alone with her.

She looked away first. "You don't have to come if you would rather do something else."

"I can't think of anything I'd rather do than go on a picnic with you. I'd love to take a long stroll around the lake."

Ada laughed. Mary didn't smile.

When Ada and Hannah left the barn, Joshua took Mary's hand again. "I'm listening now. What did you want to tell me?"

She stepped away from him. "It can wait until tomorrow. You should leave before it gets too late."

"I'm not in a hurry, Mary."

"Tomorrow. We'll talk tomorrow." She hurried out of the barn, leaving him puzzled.

Was she that worried about what she had to tell him? What could be so bad?

Chapter Thirteen

On Saturday morning, Joshua picked up Mary, Hannah, Ada and Bella for the short wagon ride to the Shetler farm. Mary sat quietly beside him. He'd spent the night wondering what she needed to tell him, determined to convince her it didn't matter. He hoped he wouldn't have to wait long to get her alone.

At the Shetler farm, they joined Joe and Naomi Shetler, along with all the Barkman sisters and their husbands and children on the shore of a small lake in Joe's pasture. The green hillsides around the lake were dotted with white sheep and playful lambs. After helping Mary and Ada out of their buggy, Joshua joined the men standing in the shade of a tall oak tree. Hannah and several of the children ran to the water's edge and threw a stick for Bella. The Lab raced in, splashing the children urging her on.

When she came out, she put the stick down and shook from head to tail. While she was busy, a large black-and-white sheepdog darted in and stole the stick and the chase was on.

Mary produced a bottle of soap and some wands and the children were soon blowing bubbles. The dogs gave up chasing each other and launched themselves at the orbs floating in the air. The other women, chatting and bustling about, were busy setting out the quilts and chairs and arranging the food on the tailgate of Joe's wagon.

Joe stroked his gray beard. "I've learned it's best to stay out of their way until they tell us it's ready."

Joshua surveyed the lake. "Is the fishing any good here?"

Nodding, Joe gestured toward the north end. "There's some mighty good fishing all along this side. Would you like a pole? I have several extras."

"I might take you up on that later." Joshua was watching Mary laughing with the children. It was good to see her so carefree.

"After you've had time to walk out with Mary, you mean." Joe chuckled.

Joshua gave him a wry smile. "Am I that obvious?"

"You forget that I've had a houseful of granddaughters all finding mates in the last two years. I know the look of a man who is smitten. Alvin and Betsy are slipping away now. You should take Mary in the other direction."

"I will. Speaking of granddaughters, I've been meaning to ask if you're related to a girl named Mary Shetler?"

"I've no relative named Mary. Why do you ask?"

"My brother knows an *Englisch* fellow who is looking for a girl by that name. Apparently, she was an old girlfriend. He thought he saw her on the television here in Hope Springs helping after the tornado."

"I'm the only Shetler in this community, but there are plenty of them over by New Philadelphia, although they are only distantly related to me. Maybe she's from one of those families. Mary is a common name. I don't know how to help you find her."

"New Philadelphia. I'll let my brother know."

"If she is Amish and left this *Englisch* fellow, it may be best that he not find her."

"I've thought of that, but they had a child together that he never met. A man should know his child."

"Perhaps this woman had a good reason for leaving him."

"Perhaps. *Danki*, Joe." Joshua saw Clara had

taken over supervising the children. Mary was strolling toward the water's edge. He left Joe chuckling behind him and went to join her.

She smiled shyly when he stopped beside her. He gazed out over the lake. Fleecy white clouds in the blue sky floated above their flawless reflections in the water, as if the beauty was too great for the heavens to hold. "This is a pretty place, don't you think?"

"*Ja*, it's peaceful here." She began walking and he fell into step beside her. He could tell she was nervous.

They strolled for a while until a bend in the shoreline took them out of view of the others.

He found a fallen log beside a blooming dogwood tree and sat down. Mary joined him.

He glanced at her sitting beside him. He wanted to kiss her more than he wanted anything else in his life. He wanted the right to hold her in his arms. In the depths of his heart, he believed she was the woman God had fashioned for him alone. It didn't matter that he wasn't her first love. It only mattered that she loved him now. He took her hand. It was small and soft and it fit his perfectly. "Mary, I have come to care deeply for you. I need to know that you feel the same."

She pulled her hand away and stood. "There are things I need to tell you before you say more. You aren't going to like hearing them."

He tried to take her hand again, but she pushed away. "Please, don't touch me. If you do, I may falter."

"I'm sorry. Mary, I don't know why you are afraid of me. I would never hurt you. Nothing you can say will change my feelings for you."

Mary wanted so much to confide in him, but she was scared. Scared it would matter. "I'm not afraid of you, Joshua. I'm afraid of the way I feel when I'm with you."

He took her hand and squeezed gently. "And how is that?"

"I feel like there might be a chance for me. A chance at happiness."

"That's how you make me feel. Why does that scare you? You deserve happiness."

"I'm afraid I'll reach for it and it will burst like one of Hannah's soap bubbles on the grass."

"There's more to it, isn't there? Is it me? Do you think I won't be back the next time I have to leave?"

"Maybe. I'm not sure."

"Why would you think that?"

"Because it has happened to me before. Hannah's father left me. The next man who took me in betrayed me, too. I've been with more than one man. I was never married, Joshua. Hannah is an illegitimate child."

"I know that."

Mary frowned. "You do? How could you know this?"

"Delbert mentioned it the first day I met him. I asked him if he knew your husband and he said he didn't think you'd ever been married but he didn't hold that against you. It is a grave matter, but it is in the past. We will never mention it again. I love you and I love Hannah."

"You've known since then?" A sob escaped her and suddenly she was crying as she hadn't cried in years. She had been so afraid and all this time he knew.

"Don't cry. It doesn't matter. I love Hannah. She is the daughter of my heart." Joshua drew Mary into his embrace and held her. He gave her his handkerchief and she cried until she didn't have any tears left.

When she grew calm, he knelt in front of her. She dried her eyes and blew her nose.

"Are you okay now?" he asked.

She had a headache and her eyes were burning as if they were full of sand, but she ignored those minor discomforts. "I'm better than I have been in a long time."

"If you are ready to go back, I'm sure they have a birthday cake for you."

"*Nee*, stay. I'm ready to tell you what happened."

"You don't have to do that."

"I do. I want you to understand what I was going through when I made some horrible decisions."

He took a seat on the tree trunk beside her. "Okay, I'm listening."

She gazed up into the beautiful sky and prayed for courage. "My father died when I was only six. I vaguely remember him. My mother remarried when I was ten. My stepfather was a good man, but he wasn't an affectionate man. He needed a wife to help him raise four sons and my mother fit the bill. I was an extra mouth to feed. My mother died in a buggy accident four years later. My stepfather didn't waste time remarrying. I never felt like I was part of the family after that."

"I'm sorry you were left alone."

"I found a job as a live-in maid with a family in Canton when I was fifteen. The husband was so nice to me. I just wanted to be loved. He saw how vulnerable I was and took advantage of that. He seduced me."

"Is he Hannah's father?"

She nodded. "When I suspected I was pregnant, I told him and I was promptly fired. He was terrified his wife would find out. I went back to my stepfather, but I wasn't welcome there. I was alone and out on the streets. I turned to my church for help, but the bishop called me terrible names. I was shunned. That's when I met someone who said he wanted to take care of my baby and me. I was so naive. You'd think I would have been smarter about men at that point, but I wasn't."

"We are taught to trust in the goodness of all men. Who was he?"

"A truly evil person. He took me in and took care of me. I thought I loved him. I began to suspect he was dealing drugs on the side, but I didn't want to believe it. I couldn't be that wrong about another person I wanted to love."

"What happened?"

"I overheard him making arrangements to sell my baby when it was born. He knew someone who would pay a lot of money for a white child. They would pay more for a son, but they would take a girl. I was sick with fear for my baby. I had nowhere to go. He made me believe I couldn't escape him."

"But you did."

"I couldn't let them have my baby. God was watching over her. I went into labor one night when he was gone and delivered Hannah by myself. I had nothing for her. I stole a quilt off the clothesline of a neighbor and wrapped her in that. I knew I had to hide her. I knew he would be back at any time. There was a convenience store not far from our place. I used to see Amish buggies parked there. There was one in the parking lot that night. I put Hannah in the basket on the backseat and I left a note begging the Amish family to take care of her. I told them to meet me in the same place in a week. I needed time to gather enough money so we could get far away from him. I believed he would find us and take her if I didn't."

"That was an incredibly brave and unselfish thing to do. Did the buggy belong to Ada?"

"*Nee*, it belonged to Levi Beachy. His brothers, Atlee and Moses, had taken it without his knowledge and met up with some girls to see a movie. They didn't know Hannah was in the backseat until they were almost home. She started crying and they panicked. They couldn't take her back. They couldn't take her home with them or their brother would know they had sneaked out without his knowledge. They were passing Ada's farm and it occurred to them that she didn't have grandchildren, so they left Hannah on her doorstep. They never saw my note. They never told anyone about her. She was found by Miriam. She saw an Amish buggy leaving and thought some unwed mother didn't want her baby. Miriam and Ada found the note and waited for me to show up at the farm. I didn't. I was in the parking lot of a convenience store praying the people I left Hannah with would bring her back. When they didn't return, I knew I'd lost her forever."

"What about the man who wanted to sell her?"

"I told him the baby was stillborn. He was furious, but he believed me. He still thought I was in love with him, but I knew I was nothing to him. I was nothing to anyone."

"That is never true. We are God's children. He is always with us, even in the dark times."

"I know that now, but I didn't believe it then. Nick and Miriam were investigating and trying to discover the identity of Hannah's family when I was taken to the hospital. I was...sick."

She wasn't ready to tell him that she had tried to end her life. She didn't have the courage. Not yet.

"Eventually, they figured out who I was and they gave Hannah back to me. I couldn't believe it. I had my baby in my arms and I had people who cared about us. Nick and Miriam were amazing. They gave me a home when they took me to live with Ada. They gave me protection and security by adopting me. God saved more than my life. He gave me a family. How can I expect anything more than that?"

"I think you are selling God short. I think He gets to decide how much joy and how much sorrow comes into our lives. His love is limitless."

Did she doubt God's mercy and goodness?

"Does Hannah's father know he has such a beautiful daughter?"

"He died in a small plane crash when she was eight months old."

"What happened to the man who wanted to sell her? I can't believe Nick would let him go unpunished. It is not the *Englisch* way to forgive."

"He was arrested for the drugs and then charged with second degree kidnapping, too, because I was a minor. It was then he learned my baby was still alive. I testified against him in court. If I hadn't, he would have gone free. I know it is not our way, but I believe he would've found another girl in trouble and sold her baby. I could not be a party to that. He made many threats against me. After only four years, he's getting out on parole. Nick and Miriam are worried that he will try to find me. That's why I was so upset about seeing my face on television." Emotionally drained and exhausted, Mary closed her eyes.

"Do you believe he will?"

"I do. That's why I changed my name to Kaufman when Miriam adopted me. It was at Nick's urging. He knew it would make it harder for Kevin Dunbar to find me. There are a lot of Mary Kaufmans among the Amish."

"Did you say Kevin Dunbar?"

The strain in Joshua's voice caused Mary to open her eyes. "Do you know him?"

Joshua rose to his feet and walked a few feet away. He raked a hand through his hair. "No, but I've heard my brother mention someone by that name. It might not be the same man. There could be more than one Kevin Dunbar in the world."

"The Kevin Dunbar I know is in the Beaumont Correctional Facility."

Joshua stared at her in shock. This could not be happening. Mary could not be the woman he had been sent to look for. He paced back and forth in front of her.

"Joshua, what's wrong?"

How much information about her had he shared? He racked his brain trying to recall all the times he had mentioned her in his letters and spoken of her when he was with Luke. Had Luke shared that information with Dunbar? Was it enough for Dunbar to figure out it was the same Mary? Maybe.

Luke was waiting for Joshua to contact him with more information. His brother needed to know Dunbar wasn't being honest with him. Joshua needed to find out exactly how much the man knew about Mary Kaufman, if anything. What if he had put her in danger?

"I know it's a lot for you to take in, Joshua. I understand that. I wouldn't blame you if you packed up and went home. I'm not exactly the kind of girl you want your parents to meet." She rose to her feet.

He stopped pacing and reached for her. "Mary, you're the only woman I'd like my parents to meet. I *am* going to pack up and go home, but I'll be back. I want you to believe that. I love you. I want us to be together, but I have to take care of something else first."

"Does it have to do with your parole?"

Joshua's jaw clenched. He had a meeting this evening with Officer Merlin at the inn. He would have to miss it. The man would be furious, but Mary was more important. Joshua had to make sure her identity was still safe.

"It's family business. It could take a couple of days. After your party, I'll catch a ride home with the man that's picking up Oscar." From there, he could get a ride with a local man to see Luke.

"But you will be back. I believe that. I love you."

He saw the soft glow in her eyes as she spoke. He pulled her into his arms and kissed her gently. "I love you, too. God willing, we will have many years to whisper those words to each other."

* * *

Joshua was shocked at the change in his brother when he visited him the following morning. Luke was hollow-eyed and shaking. "You look terrible."

"So do you. So what? What do you want?"

"I found the woman you asked me to look for. I found Mary Shetler, but you can't tell Dunbar anything about her."

Luke laughed but there wasn't any humor in it. "I didn't have to."

"What are you saying?"

"All I did was tell him my brother was courting the *Englisch* sheriff's adopted Amish daughter. I thought it was a *goot* joke considering you're on parole. Does she know that? It turns out Dunbar knows Sheriff Bradley rather well."

"Oh, Luke. You have no idea what you've done."

"I helped a friend find his daughter. Not that he turned out to be much of a friend."

"You're using again, aren't you?"

"I'm going cold turkey this time, thanks to my *goot* buddy."

"Dunbar was supplying you drugs in here? That's the kind of man you helped find an innocent woman and child?"

"Hey, keep your voice down. Do you want the guards to hear? I'm not a rat."

"Dunbar isn't Hannah's father. He tried to sell her on the black market when she was born. Mary was fifteen and homeless when he found her and took her in. Not because he cared about her, but because she was pregnant. Apparently, some people will pay large sums of money for a white baby."

Luke lost his smug look. "I don't know what you're talking about. Kevin said he was her father."

"He lied to you. Hannah's father died in an accident months after she was born. Kevin is looking for Mary because she testified against him. She's the reason he's in here."

"I didn't know any of this."

"You know what kind of man he is. You know he is dealing drugs and you would do anything for them. Did he see my letters? Does he know where she lives?"

"I'm sorry, Joshua. You have to believe that I'm sorry. He saw your letters. He was paroled two days ago."

"What is Bella barking at?" Ada looked up from her needlework.

Mary laid down the book she was reading. "I'll go see. Did Hannah come in?"

"I don't think so."

Rising from her chair, Mary went to the window to look out. There was a black car parked on their lane. Was it a driver bringing Joshua back? "I see a car at the end of the drive."

"Are they coming to the house?" Ada rose to join Mary at the window.

"*Nee*, it's just sitting there."

"Perhaps someone is lost."

"Maybe Joshua has come back." She was so eager to see him. Eager to explore the future with him.

Ada remained at the window. "I thought he said it would be several days. Now they are coming this way. You might be right."

"I'll go see." Mary hurried through the house to the kitchen door. She paused before opening the screen to still her racing heart. It might not be him. But it might be.

Bella's barking intensified, then she yelped once and was silent. Hannah screamed. Mary pushed open the screen door and rushed out. Her heart dropped to her feet when she saw Kevin standing beside the car. He had Hannah in his arms. She was struggling to get free and crying. There were two men with Kevin. Bella lay sprawled on the ground at the feet of one of them.

Mary ran toward Kevin. "Don't hurt her. I'm begging you, don't hurt my baby."

"You should have kept your mouth shut. None

of this would've happened if you had just kept your mouth shut."

Mary reached Kevin's side but one of the men stopped her when he wrapped his arms around her. She tasted the salty tears that streamed down her face. Clutching her hands together, she pleaded with Kevin, "Please, if you ever had any feelings for me at all, don't do this."

"That's just it, Mary. I never did have feelings for you. The baby was all I wanted and now I've got her. She's still worth money, although not to the same people. Tell your boyfriend I appreciate him finding you for me." He looked at his men. "Let's go."

The man holding Mary threw her to the ground. Before she could get up, they were all in the car. She grabbed the door handle, trying to reach Hannah. Her baby was screaming. Her baby needed her, but she couldn't hold on as the car drove away.

She fell to a heap in the driveway screaming Hannah's name.

Chapter Fourteen

Joshua jumped out of the van before it pulled to a stop in Ada's yard. Bella lay on the porch with her head on her paws. There was blood on the left side of her face. As soon as he saw Mary walk out of the house, his heart leaped. She was safe. He ran toward her. "Mary, I have to talk to you."

She didn't speak. She didn't move. His steps slowed as he approached her. Her face was streaked with tears. It twisted with agony. "Why did you do it? Where is she, Joshua? I can forgive anything else. Just tell me where she is."

"What are you saying? Oh, please, God, don't let it be Hannah." He caught Mary by the arms. The raw pain in her eyes was unbearable.

"He took my baby. I couldn't do anything to stop him. Why did you tell Kevin where we were?"

"I didn't, Mary. You have to believe me. I never told him anything."

Nick Bradley came out of the house. "Mary, get inside."

She ducked her head and turned away. Joshua reached for her, but Nick grabbed his arm, twisting it behind him and forcing Joshua up against the side of the house. "Joshua Bowman, you are under arrest for violating your parole and for conspiracy to commit kidnapping. You have the right to remain silent. If you give up that right, anything you say can and will be used against you in a court of law."

Joshua knew his rights. He ignored Nick as he continued to recite them and focused on Mary where she stood only a few feet away. "Mary, let me explain."

Nick jerked Joshua around. "You were in on this with Dunbar from the beginning. Where is she? Where did he take Hannah?"

"I'm not working with Kevin Dunbar. I don't expect you to believe me, but Mary, you have to believe me. I would never hurt you. I would never hurt Hannah."

"Then tell us where he took her," Nick bellowed, anger blazing in his eyes.

Joshua recoiled from the sheriff's rage. What would Nick do if he learned of Luke's part in this? Joshua didn't believe Luke had known

Kevin would harm Hannah or Mary, but he had given away their location in exchange for drugs. That alone would add years to Luke's sentence. Joshua struggled with his need to protect his brother and to find Hannah.

"I don't know where he took her." He bowed his head. He didn't expect Nick to believe him.

"Wrong answer." Nick yanked Joshua toward his SUV.

"Wait." Mary touched Nick's arm.

He stopped. "I'm not Amish. I don't get to forgive and forget. I have to uphold the law."

"I need to hear what he has to say."

Nick shook his head, but took a few steps away.

Mary placed her hand on Joshua's chest. Her heart was being torn to pieces by her frantic grief, but she knew—she knew in her soul that he was telling the truth. He loved her and he loved Hannah. She had to trust that love. If she couldn't, then she truly was a broken human being. Joshua had kept things from her, but she had kept things from him, too.

"I believe you when you say you didn't have a part in this, Joshua. I trust you. I'm sorry I accused you."

When she looked at him, his eyes were filled with tears. She loved him so much. "God sent you to save us once before. Can't you help save her now?"

Nick came to Mary's side. A tense muscle twitched in his cheek, but he had his anger under control. "Tell us what you know. I don't want to make this harder for you. I just want our little girl back."

Joshua had no choice. Hannah and Mary needed him. He had to put aside his distrust and fear of the *Englisch* law and believe that God was in charge of his fate and of Luke's. He faced Nick knowing his words might condemn his brother to more years in prison.

"I wrote home about Mary and about Hannah and their lives here. I wanted my family to know what an amazing woman she is. My mother forwarded all my letters to my brother Luke the way the Amish do with their circle letters."

Nick crossed his arms. "How did he know you were seeing Mary Shetler?"

"He didn't. Kevin saw Mary in one of the news reports about the tornado. He knew she was in Hope Springs. Luke knew I was here, too. He wrote that he needed to see me. When I went there, he told me about his friend, a guy who had been in love with an Amish girl before he went to jail. He said she was pregnant and went back to her Amish family. He saw Mary on the news. He knew she was in Hope Springs. He wanted to make sure she and his child were okay. I said I would ask around. Something about Luke's behavior bothered me. I thought he might be using drugs again, but I had no idea how he could be getting them."

Mary wiped at the tears on her face. "You never asked me about Mary Shetler."

"The only person I asked was Wooly Joe. He said what I was already thinking—that it was better to let Mary Shetler's child grow up without knowing he or she had a drug dealer for a father."

Nick pushed his hat up with one finger. "Do you think Dunbar was supplying your brother with drugs in exchange for information?"

"I can't be sure, but I think he was. I told Luke that Mary had been adopted by you. Luke thought it was hilarious—I was fresh out on parole and dating the sheriff's daughter. He shared the story with Dunbar. The man figured out that Mary Kaufman and Mary Shetler were one and the same. When Mary told me about her relationship with Dunbar, I was sick with worry that my letters would lead him here. I went to see Luke. That's why I missed my meeting with Officer Merlin. As soon as Luke told me Dunbar had been released, I came to warn you."

"Why didn't you call me?" Nick demanded. "I could have stopped him."

"Because I didn't trust you. I was afraid if you knew about Luke's dealings with Dunbar, you'd make sure he stayed in prison."

"So now Dunbar has Hannah and we're still no closer to knowing where he took her."

"Luke once mentioned Dunbar was going to set him up in business when he got out. With some of his friends in Cleveland. They're brothers who run a salvage yard."

"There are a lot of brothers in Cleveland. You're gonna have to do better than that."

"That's all I know. Luke may know more."

"You had better hope he does. He's going to tell me everything."

Joshua understood Nick's anger. "He might not talk to you, but he'll talk to me."

Nick turned to Mary. "Get your things together. You and Ada are leaving this afternoon. Miriam has a safe place for you. I want you out of harm's way in case that maniac comes back." Nick pulled open the rear door and pushed Joshua in.

"I'm coming with you. I'll be as safe with you as I am with Miriam. If Joshua's brother knows where Hannah is, maybe I can convince him to tell us."

"All right, get in."

Joshua remained silent on the long ride to the correctional facility. Mary didn't speak to him. She didn't even look at him. He could hardly blame her. She had to be terrified. The handcuffs were cutting into his wrists by the time they arrived, but he didn't complain. It was nothing more than what he deserved. Nick was right. If Joshua had only trusted Nick enough to call him, Hannah might be safe.

Mary and Joshua were seated at a wooden table when they brought Luke into the interview room. Nick leaned against the cinder-block wall. Luke wore a defiant look. "So you couldn't keep your mouth shut, little brother," he said in Pennsylvania Dutch. "You had to involve me."

"Sit down and speak English." Nick pushed away from the wall and shoved Luke into a chair. Luke glared at him.

Mary clasped her hands together on the table. "Please help us. Kevin has taken my daughter. Her name is Hannah. She is only four years old. I know she must be so frightened. I only want to get her back. Anything that you can tell us may help us find her."

Joshua added his plea. "Please, brother. I know you would never hurt a child. I know you didn't mean for any of this to happen."

Some of Luke's bluster slipped away. "I

thought he was the kid's father. A father has a right to see his child."

Nick struck the table with both hands, making everyone jump. "Do you know where he took her?"

"I don't."

Joshua said, "You told me Kevin had friends in Cleveland who would set you up with a job when you got out."

"He probably lied about that. He lied about everything else. He said he'd take care of me but the minute he got out, the supply dried up."

"Was he smuggling drugs to the inmates here?"

Luke hunched forward and rubbed his arms as if he were cold. "He still has friends inside. I can't tell you anything."

Nick pulled up a chair and sat beside Luke. "Hannah is the sweetest child you have ever met. Her eyes are as blue as the sky. She doesn't deserve to be punished because Kevin Dunbar wants to make Mary suffer. She did the right thing when she testified against him."

"I forgave him for what he tried to do to me, but I could not let him do it to someone else," she said.

Nick patted Mary's hand and then looked at Luke. "I know it will take courage to tell us what you know. Do you have as much courage as this woman does?"

Luke sat back. "The name is Sanders. They own an auto salvage lot on the west side. They've been helping Dunbar smuggle drugs into here. I don't know how. That's all I know.

"Thank you." Nick jumped up from his seat and left the room.

"Danki," Mary said, and followed him.

Joshua gave his brother a tired smile. "You did a good thing."

"It doesn't make up for all the wrong things I have done."

"Maybe not. But it's a start."

"This means I'm going to be in here for a long time."

Joshua stared at the door. "Maybe they will give us a cell together."

Perched on the end of his cot in the county jail in Millersburg, Joshua prayed, not for his release, but for Mary's and Hannah's safety. The last thing he wanted was to hurt them, and yet he had led a vicious man to their door. He didn't know how he could live with himself if anything happened to Hannah. All things were according to God's plan, but it was hard to see that when his heart was breaking.

He heard the cell-block door open. He looked

up as Sheriff Bradley paused in front of his cell. Joshua jumped to his feet. "Did you find her?"

The sheriff looked tired and worn. "My family is no concern of yours."

"I just want to know that she is safe. Please, can you tell me that much?"

Nick sighed heavily. "We found her. She's frightened but safe. We arrested two men, but Dunbar got away."

"Where is Mary now? Can I see her?"

"She and Hannah are safe with an Amish family in another community."

"Thank God." Joshua gripped the bars and laid his head against the cold steel. It didn't matter what happened to him now. He would go back to prison and finish out his sentence, but he could face that knowing they were safe.

Sheriff Bradley unlocked the cell door and held it open. "You're free to go home if you agree to follow the conditions of your original parole."

"I don't understand."

"You had a valid reason for missing your meeting with your parole officer, but it can't happen again. Do you understand?"

"Why are you doing this?"

"Because I think you love my daughter."

"I do. I love her more than life itself and I love Hannah like she was my own child."

"Then I'm sorry, but you are going to have to forget about them. They are no longer your concern. The only way to keep Mary and Hannah safe is to keep them hidden."

"If I could just say goodbye to them. That's all I'm asking. That's all I'll ever ask of you."

"No."

Hope died in Joshua's chest.

"There's a car waiting outside that will take you home."

"What about my brother? What will happen to him?"

"I'm not at liberty to talk about an ongoing case. Go home. There's nothing you can do for them."

"You have to eat something. You're going to dry up and blow away. Who will take care of Hannah then?" Ada pushed a plate piled high with meat loaf, green beans, mashed potatoes and gravy across the table to Mary.

Mary pushed it aside. "I'm not hungry, and I'm not about to dry up and blow away. I will always take care of Hannah. You should stop worrying about me."

"How can I stop worrying when there is such sadness in your eyes?"

"If you're worried that I'm going to do something stupid, don't be. I was very young and very foolish when I tried to commit suicide. I have learned that I can bear all things if I trust in the Lord. This too shall pass." They were hard words to say while her heart was breaking, but she spoke the truth.

Her daughter was safe. Bella was making a good recovery from the blow to her head. Ada hadn't suffered any ill effects from the fright and stress. It had been two weeks since Hannah's abduction and Mary had no idea if she would ever see Joshua again. She missed him dreadfully.

The outside door opened and Miriam came in. "They caught him."

Mary jumped to her feet. "They caught Kevin Dunbar?"

"He was trying to cross into Canada."

Ada patted her chest. "The goodness of the Lord be praised."

"Amen," Mary and Miriam said together, and smiled at each other.

"Does this mean we can go home?" Hannah was sitting at the table eating her green beans and dropping a few to Bella, who was on the floor at her feet.

Miriam grinned at her. "According to Papa Nick, you can."

Mary laced her fingers together and squeezed hard. "When can I see Joshua?"

"Nick is going there tomorrow. He wanted to know if you would like to go, too?"

Mary squealed in delight. "I do. I do want to go."

"Me, too," Hannah shouted.

"Me, three," Ada shouted, and they all laughed.

Miriam looked over the table. "We're to meet him there at ten o'clock. This looks good. Can I join you?"

"I will get you a plate." Ada hurried to the cupboard.

Mary sat back and gave silent thanks. The dark clouds covering her days had been blown away. If only Joshua could accept her family and her family accept him. It was a tall order, but nothing was impossible in the sight of God.

Joshua was cleaning Oscar's stall when he heard a car drive in. He put aside his pitchfork and headed to the door. It wasn't his day to meet with Officer Merlin. Who was here?

He recognized Nick Bradley's SUV and his heart thudded painfully. Were Mary and Hannah okay? Had Dunbar found them again?

Nick got out and opened the back door on the passenger's side. Joshua couldn't believe his eyes when Luke got out. He glanced toward the house. His father and mother had heard the vehicle, too, and had come outside. The joy that spilled across their faces took his breath away.

He hurried forward and held out his hand. His brother was still pale, but his eyes were clear. "Luke, I can't believe it's you. What's going on?"

"I got an early parole."

"How?"

Nick closed the door and folded his arms over his chest. "Your brother is cooperating with our investigation into drug-smuggling activities at the Beaumont Correctional Facility. In the interest of his safety, the judge has granted him parole. You might also want to know that Kevin Dunbar was arrested this morning trying to cross into Canada. He's going away for a long, long time, without the possibility of parole."

Another car turned into the drive. It was a blue sedan. Joshua didn't recognize it. By this time, all of Joshua's brothers were standing behind his parents.

Luke rubbed his palms on his pant legs. "Reckon it's time to get a tongue lashing from dear old *daed*."

Joshua slapped him on the shoulder. "It won't be as bad as you think."

As his family went into the house with Luke, Joshua stayed behind. "Was this your doing, Nick?"

"A little. I thought your family deserved a break after what happened to you."

The car pulled up behind Nick's vehicle. Joshua went weak in the knees when Hannah burst out of the backseat and came running toward him. He crouched down and gathered her in his arms. "Hannah Banana, it is so good to see you."

She squeezed his neck in a huge hug, then leaned back and patted his face with both hands. "I'm not a banana."

"I guess you aren't. You're getting to be a very big girl." Joshua put her down. He saw Miriam get out of the driver's side and open the back door. Ada got out. Then the beautiful woman he was dying to hold in his arms stepped out, too.

"Mary." He breathed her name into the air.

She slowly approached him. He'd thought about her so often, agonized over what he might say to her. Wondered what she might say to him. Now that she was standing in front of him, words failed him. He wanted to drop to his knees and beg her forgiveness.

"Hello, Joshua." Her voice was tentative, hesitant.

"Hello, Mary." He wanted to tell her how beautiful she looked in the morning light. He wanted to tell her how much he had missed the sound of her voice, the curve of her lips when she smiled, the soft blush that stained her cheeks so easily.

Miriam took Nick by the elbow and Hannah by the hand. "Let's go inside and meet Joshua's family. I'm sure they have a lot of questions for us."

Joshua shoved his hands in his pockets. He had no idea where to go from here.

Mary couldn't believe how nervous she was. Once she had Hannah safely in her arms, the only thing she'd wanted was to tell Joshua how much she missed him. Now that he was standing in front of her, she couldn't think of a thing to say. She just wanted to be in his arms. Why was he just standing there? Couldn't he see how much she loved him?

He raised his face to heaven. "When you look at me like that, I can't think straight."

"How am I looking at you?" she asked softly, stepping closer.

"Like you need me to hold you."

"I do, Joshua. I need you to hold me all the days of my life." He groaned as he pulled her close and her joy filled her to the brim. He was strong and solid—this wasn't a dream. She wouldn't wake and find she was alone in her bed in a strange house. She was finally where she belonged. She was afraid to breathe, afraid he would pull away and she would never feel this complete again. She cupped his face with her hands and gazed into his eyes. "You are a wonderful man. I don't deserve you."

He gave her a wry smile. "I'm the one who doesn't deserve you. I understand if you would rather have Delbert Miller."

Mary's heart soared as she realized her life was about to take an amazingly wonderful turn with this amazing and wonderful man. She grinned happily. "He's a fine fellow, but I think Hannah likes you better."

"What will she think about having me as a father?" His voice was hesitant. Didn't he know Hannah already loved him, too?

"She will be delighted."

"Are you sure?"

"I'm very, very sure. There's no one in the world who will be a better father than you, Joshua. I believe that with all my heart."

He brushed his lips tenderly over hers. She raised her arms to circle his neck as he crushed her close. She wanted to be held by him this way for a lifetime. When he drew away, she missed his warmth and the feel of his heart beating against hers.

Drawing a shaky breath, he said, "That still leaves one obstacle."

"I don't see any." She needed his lips on hers. She tried to pull him back, but he resisted.

"What about your father?"

"Nick? What about him?"

"Mary, my brother and I are felons. Your father is a sheriff. He's not going to like having ex-cons for in-laws. Neither will your mother."

"Oh, Joshua, you underestimate Nick and Miriam. They fell in love young, but theirs was not an easy path. Nick was English, Miriam was Amish, but there was much more. Nick was responsible for the death of Miriam's only brother."

Joshua's eyes widened with shock. "How?"

"Miriam's brother had stolen a car. He was desperate to reach the English girl he loved before she left town. Nick gave chase, not knowing who was driving the stolen vehicle. He ran the car off the road in an attempt to stop it and Miriam's brother was killed in the crash. It took a long time for Nick to forgive himself and much longer for Miriam to forgive him. A baby left on Miriam's doorstep years later brought them together."

"Hannah?"

Mary slipped her arms around Joshua's waist and laid her head on his chest. "*Ja.* It was Hannah. The baby I gave away."

When his arms closed around her, she knew

he was the one God had chosen for her. "Isn't it amazing how the Lord uses us to reach others in ways we can't imagine? Nick and Miriam understand that people make mistakes, but those mistakes do not define who we are. What we do with each new day that God gives us defines who we are in His sight."

"In that case, Mary Kaufman, will you marry me? I love you. I don't want to face a life without you. Every morning and every night I want my love for you to define who I am in the sight of God."

Sweet bliss filled her heart and surged through her veins. She hated doing it, but he had to know one more thing before she gave him her answer. She stepped back and pulled up her sleeve. Her scars stood out puckered and white on her wrists. "You know what these are from?"

"I don't, but it must have hurt you very much."

"I don't remember it hurting. I did it to myself, Joshua. I tried to kill myself with a broken piece of bathroom mirror. I cut my wrists open and waited to die."

She expected the shock she saw in his face, but she hadn't expected how quickly his expression changed to compassion. "You must have been terribly alone."

It was so long ago, but she could feel the cold creeping over her even now the way it had as she lay dying. "You can't know what it's like to reach the point where you believe in your soul that you and everyone else will be better off if you're dead. After I lost Hannah, I had nothing to live for. I wasn't sick when Nick and Miriam found me in the hospital. I tried to commit suicide."

He caressed her cheek with his fingers. "I'm sorry you went through such a terrible ordeal, but I rejoice that your life was spared. Mary, it doesn't change the way I feel when I'm with you."

"Truly?"

"Truly."

She let out the breath she had been holding. "In that case, I would love to marry you."

He pulled her close and kissed her again, with infinite tenderness and passion. Mary saw just how wonderful their life together was going to be.

The door to the house opened and Hannah came out with a cookie in her hand. "Joshua, your mother is a *goot* cook."

"I'm glad you think so." He picked her up and sat her on the hood of Nick's SUV. "Hannah, I have a serious question for you."

"I haven't blamed Bella for anything she didn't do."

He glanced at Mary and chuckled. "I'm glad

to hear that. I need your permission for something important. I would like to marry your mother. What do you think about that?"

Her mouth fell open. "I thought you were going to marry me?"

"I love you dearly, but your mother is already twenty. This might be her last chance to get a husband."

Hannah thought it over, and then nodded. "Okay. Can I get another cookie?"

Laughing, Joshua took one of her hands and Mary took the other. They swung her off the hood and walked into their future together.

* * * * *

Dear Readers,

It is with a certain sadness that I have ended my Brides of Amish Country series. The tranquility of the Amish country near Hope Springs has been a wonderful getaway for many of you, and for me, too. I honestly think I could have gone on and on writing about the people there, but then I met a new fellow.

When I first started writing about Joshua Bowman, he was an only child. Then I gave him a troubled brother, and I gave him an older brother. And finally I gave him two younger brothers. The five sons of Isaac Bowman all deserve a chance at love and happiness. Joshua proved that he deserved love in this story. I fear that Luke will have a much more difficult time. With that thought in mind, the first book in my new series will be about Samuel, the oldest and the most stalwart of the sons.

I am certain that characters from Hope Springs will make their way to Bowmans Crossing for the occasional visit, wedding celebration and community gathering. After all, they are only a day's buggy ride apart.

Thanks for exploring Amish country with me.
Sincerely,

Patricia Davids

LARGER-PRINT BOOKS!

GET 2 FREE
LARGER-PRINT NOVELS
PLUS 2 FREE
MYSTERY GIFTS

Love Inspired®
SUSPENSE
RIVETING INSPIRATIONAL ROMANCE

Larger-print novels are now available...

YES! Please send me 2 FREE LARGER-PRINT Love Inspired® Suspense novels and my 2 FREE mystery gifts (gifts are worth about $10). After receiving them, if I don't wish to receive any more books, I can return the shipping statement marked "cancel." If I don't cancel, I will receive 4 brand-new novels every month and be billed just $5.24 per book in the U.S. or $5.74 per book in Canada. That's a savings of at least 23% off the cover price. It's quite a bargain! Shipping and handling is just 50¢ per book in the U.S. and 75¢ per book in Canada.* I understand that accepting the 2 free books and gifts places me under no obligation to buy anything. I can always return a shipment and cancel at any time. Even if I never buy another book, the two free books and gifts are mine to keep forever.

110/310 IDN F5CC

Name _____ (PLEASE PRINT) _____

Address _____ Apt. #

City _____ State/Prov. _____ Zip/Postal Code

Signature (if under 18, a parent or guardian must sign)

Mail to the **Harlequin® Reader Service:**
IN U.S.A.: P.O. Box 1867, Buffalo, NY 14240-1867
IN CANADA: P.O. Box 609, Fort Erie, Ontario L2A 5X3

Are you a current subscriber to Love Inspired Suspense books
and want to receive the larger-print edition?
Call 1-800-873-8635 or visit www.ReaderService.com.

* Terms and prices subject to change without notice. Prices do not include applicable taxes. Sales tax applicable in N.Y. Canadian residents will be charged applicable taxes. Offer not valid in Quebec. This offer is limited to one order per household. Not valid for current subscribers to Love Inspired Suspense larger-print books. All orders subject to credit approval. Credit or debit balances in a customer's account(s) may be offset by any other outstanding balance owed by or to the customer. Please allow 4 to 6 weeks for delivery. Offer available while quantities last.

Your Privacy—The Harlequin® Reader Service is committed to protecting your privacy. Our Privacy Policy is available online at www.ReaderService.com or upon request from the Harlequin Reader Service.

We make a portion of our mailing list available to reputable third parties that offer products we believe may interest you. If you prefer that we not exchange your name with third parties, or if you wish to clarify or modify your communication preferences, please visit us at www.ReaderService.com/consumerschoice or write to us at Harlequin Reader Service Preference Service, P.O. Box 9062, Buffalo, NY 14269. Include your complete name and address.

LISLPDIR13R

REQUEST YOUR FREE BOOKS!

2 FREE WHOLESOME ROMANCE NOVELS IN LARGER PRINT

PLUS 2
FREE
MYSTERY GIFTS

⁂⁂⁂⁂⁂⁂⁂⁂⁂⁂⁂⁂⁂⁂⁂⁂⁂⁂⁂

HEARTWARMING™

⁂⁂⁂⁂⁂⁂⁂⁂⁂⁂⁂⁂⁂⁂⁂⁂⁂⁂⁂

Wholesome, tender romances

YES! Please send me 2 FREE Harlequin® Heartwarming Larger-Print novels and my 2 FREE mystery gifts (gifts worth about $10). After receiving them, if I don't wish to receive any more books, I can return the shipping statement marked "cancel." If I don't cancel, I will receive 4 brand-new larger-print novels every month and be billed just $4.99 per book in the U.S. or $5.74 per book in Canada. That's a savings of at least 23% off the cover price. It's quite a bargain! Shipping and handling is just 50¢ per book in the U.S. and 75¢ per book in Canada.* I understand that accepting the 2 free books and gifts places me under no obligation to buy anything. I can always return a shipment and cancel at any time. Even if I never buy another book, the two free books and gifts are mine to keep forever.

161/361 IDN F47N

Name _____ (PLEASE PRINT)

Address _____ Apt. #

City _____ State/Prov. _____ Zip/Postal Code

Signature (if under 18, a parent or guardian must sign)

Mail to the **Harlequin® Reader Service:**
IN U.S.A.: P.O. Box 1867, Buffalo, NY 14240-1867
IN CANADA: P.O. Box 609, Fort Erie, Ontario L2A 5X3

* Terms and prices subject to change without notice. Prices do not include applicable taxes. Sales tax applicable in N.Y. Canadian residents will be charged applicable taxes. Offer not valid in Quebec. This offer is limited to one order per household. Not valid for current subscribers to Harlequin Heartwarming larger-print books. All orders subject to credit approval. Credit or debit balances in a customer's account(s) may be offset by any other outstanding balance owed by or to the customer. Please allow 4 to 6 weeks for delivery. Offer available while quantities last.

Your Privacy—The Harlequin® Reader Service is committed to protecting your privacy. Our Privacy Policy is available online at www.ReaderService.com or upon request from the Harlequin Reader Service.

We make a portion of our mailing list available to reputable third parties that offer products we believe may interest you. If you prefer that we not exchange your name with third parties, or if you wish to clarify or modify your communication preferences, please visit us at www.ReaderService.com/consumerchoice or write to us at Harlequin Reader Service Preference Service, P.O. Box 9062, Buffalo, NY 14269. Include your complete name and address.

HWDIR13R

ReaderService.com

Manage your account online!

- Review your order history
- Manage your payments
- Update your address

> ### *We've designed the Harlequin® Reader Service website just for you.*

Enjoy all the features!

- Reader excerpts from any series
- Respond to mailings and special monthly offers
- Discover new series available to you
- Browse the Bonus Bucks catalog
- Share your feedback

Visit us at:
ReaderService.com